SF Books by Vaughn Heppner

DOOM STAR SERIES:
Star Soldier
Bio Weapon
Battle Pod
Cyborg Assault
Planet Wrecker
Star Fortress
Task Force 7 (Novella)

EXTINCTION WARS SERIES:
Assault Troopers
Planet Strike
Star Viking
Fortress Earth

INVASION AMERICA SERIES:
Invasion: Alaska
Invasion: California
Invasion: Colorado
Invasion: New York
Invasion: China

Visit www.Vaughnheppner.com for more information.

Task Force 7
(Doom Star 7)

by
Vaughn Heppner

Copyright © 2017 by the author.

This book is a work of fiction. Names, characters, places and incidents are either products of the author's imagination or used fictitiously. Any resemblance to actual events, locales or persons, living or dead, is entirely coincidental. All rights reserved. No part of this publication can be reproduced or transmitted in any form or by any means, without permission in writing from the author.

ISBN-13: 978-1544971322
ISBN-10: 154497132X
BISAC: Fiction / Science Fiction / Military

-1-

Day 752: Sub-sergeant Mule and Sergeant Chen sweated in a workout room aboard Mothership *Slovakia*.

Like a caged rat, Mule ran on a circular wheel. He had short hair, hard eyes and harder muscles. Indications of a ruthless fighting mentality showed in his demeanor. He was the squad's sniper and scout. Today, he sweated as the odometer clicked onto six kilometers.

Chen performed curls, using an excessive amount of cable resistance. The Marine's biceps swelled with blood. He had wide, flat features and possessed enormous strength. After finishing the set, the sergeant mopped his face with a towel.

"Have you heard the latest?" Chen was privy to more information than most. He went into officer country at times, which was on a different part of the mothership.

"Earth news?" Mule asked.

"Yeah, right," Chen said sarcastically. "I have Task Force 7 news. Are you interested?"

They were part of Task Force 7: two *Engels*-class strike cruisers and a *Trotsky*-class mothership. They headed for a cyborg-occupied planetoid named Tyche. It was in the Oort cloud and they had already taken two years travel time to reach this far. That made this the longest combat mission in human history.

There had been a monstrous, destructive war in the Solar System until Marten Kluge had ended it by using the sunbeam. Thousands of near-Sun mirrors had fed a gigantic focusing lens that fired a massive, annihilating ray. Because of Kluge, the newly-forged Alliance had won, but still mopped up stubborn cyborg strongholds throughout the system.

Task Force 7 had a singular and dangerous assignment to perform in the distant Oort cloud. They were going because the sunbeam couldn't reach past Pluto.

"Any time you're ready to talk," Mule said, as he continued to run on the wheel.

Mule was a strange one even for a Marine. His passion ran deep, to the very fibers of his soul. During the war, the cyborgs had killed or converted everyone on Mars, an entire civilization. Mule's people were gone, including his wife, kids and parents. Mule had survived because he'd been a Martian secret service agent once. He'd protected a Martian diplomat on Earth. That had ended with his planet's death. He'd joined the Alliance Space Marines because he wanted one thing: to hunt cyborgs, and especially, to kill them. Doing so wouldn't bring back the dead, but it would stoke the fires that raged in his heart.

"I don't know when Command intends telling the rest of the Marines," Chen was saying. "So you'll have to keep this quiet for now."

Mule nodded.

Chen hesitated, maybe reconsidering. He glanced into various corners of the workout chamber, as if searching for eavesdroppers.

Mule waited. He was patient.

Finally, in a low voice, Chen said, "Strike Cruiser *Ashurbanipal* has left the flotilla."

"What?"

"Crazy, isn't it?"

A cold anger tightened Mule's features. These were elite crews and the best Marines. The Alliance didn't have many ships left. Everyone knew that sending three warships all the way to Tyche had caused bitter debates among the leadership. Now one crew had broken and mutinied?

"Is this information reliable?" Mule asked.

"Command fears to tell the boys," Chen said. "But they'll have to say something soon before word leaks out and starts a panic."

With his thoughts in turmoil, Mule began to sprint on the wheel. He was the lone Martian among the Earthers who made up *Slovakia's* Marines and crew. The Earthborn practiced different customs than he did and sometimes he rubbed the others the wrong way.

His physique highlighted much of that difference. He was lean like all Martians—lean as they *used* to be. Despite his muscles, his ribs showed, making him seem like a starvation victim.

Most of the Earthborn Marines took synthetic, performance-enhancing drugs that changed the body. One was called *Dense*, a muscle-building aid considerably more powerful than old-fashioned steroids. Another was *Quake*, which speeded neural impulses, making the user faster, if more irritable. The worst sin in Mule's view was the posthypnotic hate-conditioning given to the Marines. Because of the enforced emotion, he feared his fellow warriors would act too rashly in combat and unnecessarily get themselves killed before completing the task of destroying the enemy.

Mule hated the enemy too, but his was a cold and lethal thing guided by intellect. He would do anything to kill cyborgs, but he intended on staying alive a long time so he could destroy more of the foul melds.

The wheel's odometer clicked onto seven kilometers. Mule slowed down and he noticed a droplet of sweat floating before him. He picked up a towel and wiped himself down. He didn't want more sweat to detach from his skin, float around the chamber and clog the recyclers.

"When did *Ashurbanipal* mutiny?" Mule asked.

"Five days ago," Chen said. "The ringleaders contacted our captain and told him this was a suicide mission. We learned three days ago that the mutineers killed *Ashurbanipal's* captain and his Marine guards. But they began braking five days ago. They're already hundreds of thousands of kilometers behind us."

"Didn't *Belisarius* attack *Ashurbanipal*?" Mule asked.

"They couldn't risk it," Chen said. "The ringleaders knew what they were doing and had every missile and gun radar-locked on *Belisarius*. If the other strike cruiser would have attempted battle, the best we could have hoped for would have been mutual annihilation."

"They were supposed to be an elite crew," Mule said. "*Ashurbanipal* was our best ship."

"The odds are getting longer, that's for sure."

Mule's stomach tightened. This had happened five days ago. Five days… *Slovakia* hadn't begun braking maneuvers yet. That meant they were still heading toward Tyche. Would Captain Han suddenly quit and decide to turn around?

"This is a disaster," Mule said.

"Agreed," Chen said. "We need *Ashurbanipal's* firepower to tackle the cyborgs."

"What?" Mule asked. "Oh. Right, you're right, we need more firepower."

Chen stared at him and finally shook his head. "You're worried this will jeopardize our mission and that we'll go home. You're not really thinking about what this means: that we're lacking a badly needed warship."

"Do you want to turn back?" Mule asked.

"When I'm in the right mood in my bunk and thinking clearly, yeah, then I realize I'd love to go back home. This *is* a suicide mission. The rest of the time the hate-conditioning takes hold and all I can think about is crushing cyborg skulls."

"You don't own your hate," Mule said.

"What?"

Your hate owns you. For maybe the first time since heading to Tyche, Mule felt sorry for his brother in arms.

"As long as we have surprise we'll be okay," Mule said.

"Keep telling yourself that," Chen said. "Maybe you'll actually believe it."

Mule continued running. The Marines exercised for hours every day. Otherwise, the extended weightlessness would leech their strength and stamina and leave them too weak to destroy the cyborgs.

The reason for the task force had come from the last Neptunian humans alive—scientists on Tyche. A scientist on the Oort cloud planetoid had sent a distress signal. It had been one word long, a scream of, *"Cyborgs!"*

Mule had heard a recording of the message; they all had. He'd heard the terror in the man's voice and it had sent his heart pounding. He'd envisioned his wife and children screaming like that when the cyborgs had invaded their underground city on Mars. Just like on Mars, the cyborgs had slaughtered or converted every human living in the Neptune gravitational system, including the various moons and space habitats.

Mule had seen gruesome videos of what happened to men and women caught by cyborgs. It was brutal, sick and irreversible. To a cyborg, a human was a meat-sack of valuable body-parts.

The cyborgs, or melds, had it down to a science, an assembly-line horror. They used skin-peelers to pull away the outer epidermis and fine-tuned saws to tease off the muscles of a captured human. It was the spine and the brain that counted to the cyborgs, and the eyes and other hard-to-manufacture parts. The melds married human material to machines as if it were cloth, making synthetic demons, more cyborgs. His wife and children—

Mule shook his head.

One word screamed from the scientist on Tyche, from one of the few survivors of Neptunian civilization. Mule had heard a recording of the short message. The first time, he recalled staring at the speakers, waiting for more. There had been heavy breathing, a background explosion, an intake of air from a living being and then hard static. "Cyborgs!" had been the only and last word to transmit from the science station on Tyche concerning the subject of melds.

Because of the stellar distance, the one-word message sent by laser beam had almost been a year old by the time Marten Kluge received it.

Over two years ago, *Slovakia* and two strike cruisers had peeled away from the Alliance Armada headed for the Jupiter gravitational system. Humanity was on the offensive, hunting the cyborgs. With Kluge sun-beaming anything that moved in space, the armada could concentrate on each meld-controlled

Jupiter moon and habitat. If the cyborgs proved too stubborn in a particular place, the sunbeam sliced and diced the moon into tiny chunks. Io at Jupiter was already gone, as was Triton in the Neptune system.

Task Force 7 had built up sufficient velocity and over a year ago, each ship had shut off its fusion drive. The ships were coasting the rest of the way to Tyche, cloaked in silence and stealth. The idea was to surprise the cyborgs.

"You're certain we're continuing the mission?" Mule asked.

"If we were going to stop," Chen said, "the captain would have already begun to brake."

Mule's stomach began to loosen.

Not only did Marten Kluge possess the sunbeam, but also the giant interferometer that swept the Solar System searching for stealthy cyborg ships. If that wasn't enough, the Alliance had deployed over a hundred drones throughout the Outer Planets to watch for secretive cyborg stealth craft, for the hated Lurkers. That was the cyborg signature: to sneak in close and attack out of the darkness.

Despite the drone surveillance and the giant interferometer, at least one Lurker had reached Tyche. Because of that, the rulers of the Solar System feared for the future. Task Force 7 was the answer, and despite losing one-third of the flotilla to mutiny, it looked as if it would continue to be.

-2-

Day 993: Two hundred and forty-one days after learning about *Ashurbanipal's* defection, Mule rested his forehead against the plexiglass of a ship observatory. He raised his hands, pressing his fingertips and palms against the cold plastic.

The giant star Sirius ahead of *Slovakia* had become the brightest object in space. This far out, the Sun was only the third-brightest star. Alpha Centauri off below the ecliptic and to the side had become the second brightest.

Task Force 7 traveled in the Oort cloud, the great halo of objects around the Solar System. Tyche was an anomaly here, a freak. The dirty little ice balls making up the halo were comet-like things, floating or orbiting in the most frozen reaches of the Solar System, varying from 2,000 to 200,000 AUs from the Sun.

The Oort cloud was the last frontier, the final place under the influence of Sol's gravity.

These distances meant that once Task Force 7 reached fifty thousand AUs, they would be one-quarter of the way to Proxima Centauri, the nearest star to Sol.

It means we're all alone out here, with no one to help us.

Tyche orbited about 56,000 AUs from Earth, almost a light-year away. One light-year was a little over 62,000 AUs.

Mule often came to the observatory to think about his dead wife and children. He still desperately missed them. He was alone now, a mote of breathing life burning for vengeance. He wanted to mouth, "I love you," to his departed wife. Today, he couldn't do it. She was gone, and so far away on Mars, so far...

Unable to bear the ache of loneliness, he turned to go. The simple act of turning his head saved his eyesight. A blinding flash lit up the observation deck and cast Mule's shadow against the far wall.

Instinctively, he threw himself onto the floor, surging to the hatch, slithering through and shutting it behind him.

Klaxons began to wail with loud and piercing noises. Did it signal a cyborg attack on the task force?

Ship speakers crackled into life. Through them, a man cleared his throat. "This is Captain Han speaking. Every crewmember and Marine will immediately report to his quarters. I say again, report to your quarters. This is no drill, report to your quarters at once."

Mule grabbed a float-rail, pulling himself along the steel corridor. Other Marines around him did likewise. His heart hammered and he found himself short of breath. *We can't be anywhere near Tyche yet. What just happened?*

From within his quarters, Mule heard the captain's explanation several hours later. Over loudspeakers, Han assured the crew that no enemy drone or missile had struck them. Sabotage from within Strike Cruiser *Belisarius* had caused that vessel's destruction.

Chen sneered at that. Mule silently agreed with the Marine's sentiment, finding the news hard to believe. Command was covering up something.

During the next few days, Marines talked about *Belisarius's* faulty fusion core. The men had known about it beforehand, even though Command had tried to keep it a secret. Keeping anything quiet was hard to do when they were all alone out here. Maybe the faulty core had finally ruptured and gone critical. Whatever the case, everyone aboard the strike cruiser was dead and gone.

Through the process of elimination, Mothership *Slovakia* had become the sole vessel of Task Force 7. There wasn't any question of turning back, not in the chain of command's minds. Mule heard Marines whispering the idea to each other, but nothing came of it; certainly no mutiny brewed.

Perhaps as bad—although Captain Han didn't mention it—the cyborgs on Tyche might have detected the blast. If the melds had seen it, they might know someone was approaching their base. The Alliance mothership was still months away from Tyche and extremely small in stellar terms, less than a pinprick. It was very possible the cyborgs hadn't noticed the explosion and still had no idea of the coming attack.

Mule lay on his cot thinking about it. His knowledge of combat tactics had matured from his late-night studying. Space battle was quite different from secret service details.

He'd come to realize that the right way to conduct this assault would have been with battleships, heavy cruisers and dropships. The battleships and heavy cruisers would fight their way past enemy missiles, lasers and gun tubes. A battleship's giant particle shields would absorb damage while the long-range beams took out the enemy's offensive weaponry. Then, and only then, would armored dropships bring Marines near, racing down to gain a foothold on the surface.

Instead, Task Force 7 had a mothership, which they dare not risk to enemy fire. If *Slovakia* exploded like *Belisarius*, they had no way back home. Would Kluge send a badly needed cruiser for Marines stranded on Tyche? That would mean the warship would be out of action for six years. The conflict back home was still too bitter to detach a cruiser for six long years just for the sake of a few men.

How many cyborgs were on Tyche anyway? How heavy were their defenses? Did they have missile launch pits? Did the melds possess laser batteries or proton beams?

Mule had no idea. No one did, but he figured he would find out in another few months.

***

Day 1089: Mule played Fist Ball against Hayes, one of his squad-mates. They stood in a centrifugal chamber, each man wearing padded gloves.

"Nine to two," Hayes said.

The high-pitched whine of the churning centrifugal chamber changed suddenly, slowing.

"Wait a minute," Mule said.

Hayes looked up. He was big and beefy with the customary wide Marine features. "Who's doing that?"

"I am," Chen said over a loudspeaker.

Mule and Hayes traded glances.

Soon, the chamber stopped rotating and everything became weightless. The hatch opened and Chen beckoned them outside.

"What's up, Sarge?" Hayes asked, pulling himself into the corridor.

Chen pointed at a wall speaker.

"I hope I have everyone's attention," Captain Han's voice said from it.

"It's a ship-wide message," Chen said. "I thought you'd want to hear it."

Mule's spine tingled. Mothership *Slovakia* was eight days from Tyche and due to begin braking maneuvers in six. Perhaps they would finally get some answers.

From the speaker, Captain Han cleared his throat. "Crew, Space Marines, I have solemn news to report. We have spotted five enemy missiles headed our way. They originated from a region between Tyche and us. At present velocities, the missiles are seven days out. We must assume the possibility that they will increase acceleration and shorten the time to contact with us."

"It wasn't supposed to work like that," Hayes complained. "We've spent three painful years sneaking up on them. Damn that faulty fusion core."

Mule nodded. The cyborgs must have seen the blast after all.

"Space Marines," the captain said. "You will report to the hanger bays in twenty minutes, as there has been a change in operational plans. That is all."

***

Mule sat with a couple hundred Marines packed onto Hanger Deck C. Around him squatted bruisers with thick necks, bristling hair and bulging triceps. Most had aggressive-looking tattoos of predatory animals or harsh sayings printed in block letters, and every one of them wore green tee shirts that showed their ripped bodies.

His fellow Marines squatted or sat, cracking their knuckles, scratching itches and watching the briefing officer with their hate-shining eyes. Mention cyborgs and these warriors started snarling. Several pumped meaty fists into the air. Others shouted vicious slogans laced with curses and mayhem-filled promises.

The tall briefing officer with his hologram clicker grinned back at the Marines, but Mule could feel the man's discomfort. The officer twitched too much and he checked his chronometer far too often. That was the wrong way to act here.

Mule understood the Navy slug's discomfort. It must be like standing in a cage with man-eating tigers watching him. The Marines hungrily absorbed his words, their thick necks craning, showing the muscles and the heavy veins. The battle-lust shining on their faces caused some to inch closer to the officer.

The reason for the posthypnotic conditioning was clear to Mule. Hate the enemy so you didn't fear him. If you feared, you hesitated, and hesitating against a meld was certain death. Cyborgs fought with insectile speed. To see one fully, you had to wait until it stopped or moved with exaggerated slowness. And they were strong as well. Cyborgs had graphite-powered bones, synthetic muscles and armored bodies. They could punch through bulkheads and rip a man in two. Even with injections of *Dense* and an accelerated weightlifting schedule, a man was no match in strength, nor would he ever be as fast as a cyborg. Marines had to rely on teamwork, discipline and firepower to beat their cybernetic enemies.

With the click of his thumb, the briefing officer changed the holoimage.

A round object appeared in the air. It was a holoimage of Tyche. Two thousand and fifty-three kilometers in diameter, it was a rocky planetoid with lots of methane ice on the surface. There had been an ancient theory that suggested Tyche would prove to be a gas giant in the Oort cloud. The theory had been wrong.

"The captain has used the ship's telescopes," the Navy slug told them. "So far, he has been unable to find any Lurkers. We have, however, found this."

The briefing officer clicked his device and a new holoimage appeared. It showed a vast exhaust port many tens of kilometers wide for a drive engine. The thing was built into the planetoid, a gargantuan construct. The Neptunians might have built it, but it seemed more likely the cyborgs had done so.

Throughout the war, the cyborgs had used several operational strategies. One of their favorite had been raining asteroids on targeted planets or moons. To achieve the proper velocity with their billion-ton missiles, the cyborgs had built mammoth fusion engines into their asteroids. If they had also built the port, there must be more cyborgs here than expected.

"We're uncertain what the cyborgs hope to achieve with such a monstrous moving planetoid," the briefing officer said. "Some of our scientists believe the melds will conform to their normal strategies. That means they will attempt to turn the planetoid into a huge invasion platform, perhaps to take out the sunbeam. Tyche is far enough out to build up a high velocity before the sunbeam could strike it with annihilating power. Still, much of Tyche is composed of methane ice, and the sunbeam could quickly burn it down to the core. We suspect most of the cyborg habitats are buried in the ice. Such a burn-off would destroy the living quarters.

"Other scientists disagree with the majority view. The cyborgs are rational and logical, they say. The melds have lost the war and have no desire to die in an illogical blaze of glory. But if they aren't building Tyche as an attack platform, to gather their last soldiers in one final assault, what are they doing? A minority group of scientists believes the planetoid could act as a giant generational vessel, able to support hundreds of thousands of individuals as it crossed interstellar space to a new star system. That would mean the cyborgs are escaping our system, perhaps to begin the war anew in some distant future.

"The truth is that we don't know what they plan to do with the planetoid," the briefing officer continued. "Whatever their objective, we're here to stop them. In several hours, the captain will launch the assault torpedoes. We're doing that *before* the cyborg missiles reach this mothership. There are two good reasons for that. One, if *Slovakia* is destroyed, you Marines will still be able to complete the mission. Two, without the torpedoes attached to the mothership, *Slovakia* will be more maneuverable and more likely to survive the enemy attack. Are there any questions before I begin the tactical objectives?"

Surprisingly, there were none. Like Mule, the Marines were ready to fight.

The briefing officer nodded, clicked the device and began to outline objectives.

-3-

Launch hour arrived. *Slovakia* was six days out from Tyche. Eight days if one counted the hard braking that needed to occur for the mothership to land on the planetoid.

While thinking about it, Mule donned his powered armor. Five cyborg missiles accelerated for *Slovakia*. The mothership bored in toward Tyche. Those missiles hadn't lifted from the icy surface. According to the briefing officer, they had been drifting in space like proximity mines.

Whether the five missiles had radar-alerted fuses or cyborg fingers pushing buttons didn't matter. The five big missiles had announced their presence by the long fusion tails reaching far behind them, by accelerating at the mothership.

The enemy missiles homed in on *Slovakia*. Therefore it was time to launch the Marines before the next cyborg move announced itself.

There were many possible ways to place troops onto a planetoid surface. The cyborgs liked using black-ice coated projectiles, making them nearly radar-invisible and teleoptic-proof. A more common way was by using dropships to deploy suited Marines, or by simply landing on the surface in shuttles and disembarking. *Slovakia's* captain had ordered use of torpedoes.

Mule and his squad-mates donned powered armor. These represented the latest development in Marine hardware, very similar to the best Highborn suits.

The battlesuit's exoskeleton amplified a wearer's strength, while biphase carbide plates with shock-absorbing padding protected the Marine inside. Its helmet had an integral sensor visor and holographic HUD. Computers assisted with targeting and other functions. The suit was airtight and pressurized for vacuum.

These battlesuits also had chameleon systems to change color to match the background. As a further advantage, the chameleon systems dampened heat and infrared signatures.

Each of them carried gyroc smart rifles. The rifle fired a .75 caliber, spin-stabilized rocket. Against cyborgs, they used Armor Piercing Exploding, APEX, rounds. The smart rounds were actually tiny guided missiles, able to make course corrections to stay on target. Each squad also had a heavy weapon, a tripod-mounted flamer. It fired superhot plasma, a short-range blast that killed whatever it hit, with no exceptions.

"How many days are we going to be in the torpedoes again?" Hayes asked Chen.

"Load up with plenty of vids and other entertainment," Chen said. "It will be at least six days before we touch down."

Mule wore a slick-suit inside the powered armor. It helped keep him at a comfortable temperature.

His squad had five Marines, including their leader, Sergeant Chen. Mule was the squad sniper and scout. His suit was faster and not quite as heavily armored as the others' were. His chameleon systems were much more extensive, though, so his battlesuit ended up weighing the same as the others.

Early on, armorers had individually fitted each suit to the wearer. Six or more days inside one of these meant it was going to get rank and scratchy. There were stims, *Quake* and slowdown drugs in the suit's integral med-kit. There was extra ammo, replacement battery packs and recyclers. It made for a bulky load.

Now an armorer helped Mule secure his helmet. His breath bounced back against his face, causing a momentary feeling of claustrophobia. To break his funk, Mule began testing systems, turning on each of the suit's computers in sequence. Ten minutes later, he confirmed everything was in order. So did the others of their squad.

"Follow me," a Navy lieutenant said.

The man had just come from officer country. He wore the new Navy blues of the Alliance Fleet. Mule felt like an overfed gorilla as he clanked after the lieutenant. He dwarfed the man, and if he wanted, Mule could have twisted the lieutenant in two.

Just like a cyborg could do to us.

His suit's motors were set on ultra-low power and they moved through a narrow steel corridor. The lieutenant opened a hatch, and Mule's gut crawled with emotions.

The squad had often practiced outside *Slovakia*'s hull, in space. The mothership even towed a gunnery cage, and Mule had used it many times to drill. This was different. This might be the last time he ever walked the corridors of *Slovakia*.

The lieutenant pushed through the hatch and floated down a flexible tube. Mule switched off magnetic power to his boots, pushed and floated after the man. He could see the stars outside, and by peering just right, he saw their destination—a Phoenix assault torpedo.

The core of the mothership was rather small, as such things went. It contained life-support and crew quarters. Everything else was outside *Slovakia*. On racks, it carried the Phoenix torpedoes and Electron drones. The mothership lacked the particle shields—asteroid-like rock—that battleships and strike cruisers kept in front of them. Instead, *Slovakia* depended on keeping its distance from the fight and if needed, spraying lead-laced gels and prismatic crystals before it.

Mule didn't know how gels or crystals were going to stop the five missiles. The captain would have to use the laser or fire anti-missile rockets. But those were big missiles headed this way, each one a quarter the size of *Slovakia*. Who knew what defensive systems each enemy missile possessed?

The mothership was like a giant spider web, with the egg sac in the center, the life-support areas. Instead of cocooned flies and other bugs, the web held torpedoes and drone missiles.

The lieutenant opened another hatch, and then he led them into their torpedo, a small, cramped chamber.

"It's cold in here," the lieutenant said.

Mule's outer suit sensors picked up his words. The sensors also told him it was forty-one degrees in the chamber.

The Phoenix had a big bulbous head. Most of that was plate armor and ECM equipment. The rest held crew space and firing tubes.

Mule watched as the lieutenant began to open smaller hatches. The hatches were embedded on a bulkhead in a half-moon arrangement. The hatches led to five pod beds.

"In you go," the lieutenant announced in much too cheery a voice.

For a moment, none of the Marines moved.

Mule found that interesting. Even with hate-conditioning—

"The sooner you go in," the lieutenant told them, "the sooner you'll get to kill cyborgs."

"Right," Chen said. "Hop in, boys."

Four Marines pushed headfirst into four different pod hatches. Above each hatch was stenciled a name.

"Sub-sergeant," the lieutenant said to Mule. "Don't you want to kill cyborgs?"

The Navy slug peered at him with a smirk on his narrow face. Of course, he was using the conditioning, trying to hurry them along through bloodlust.

Mule had never trusted the hate-conditioning. As a scout and sniper, he didn't have the posthypnotic commands embedded in him. He feared the conditioning would make the others too rash in battle. Even less, he didn't like this Navy officer *using* the conditioning against his friends. A man should own his hate, not have it foisted upon him.

"How about I shove you into my hole?" Mule asked.

The Navy officer blinked rapidly, with surprise.

Mule lifted his arms and took a step toward the man. It brought a smile to his lips, because the manipulative slug flinched away. The lieutenant actually blanched white when his back hit the bulkhead.

"Don't *you* want to kill cyborgs?" Mule asked.

The lieutenant opened his mouth, but he didn't seem able to speak.

"We've traveled three years to do this," Mule said. "The least you can do is to give us a little respect."

The Navy slug nodded, and he wasn't smirking anymore. In fact, he was frightened, maybe getting ready to crap his nice clean pants.

Mule shrugged, causing his exoskeleton motor to purr with power.

"Have a good life, sir," Mule said. Then he, too, went in head first into his hatch. It became dark and he heard a clang. The lieutenant must have closed his hatch first.

The five hatches led to five pod beds. Each of the beds would cocoon the person in it. At the right time, the torpedo would fire each Marine through its nosecone in a special insertion pod toward Tyche's surface. The torpedo was like a flying shotgun and the Marine pods were the shells.

Mule found his pod, lay in it and began hooking cables to the outer ports in the suit. The cables would supply him with food, air and warmth, and dispose of his wastes. He made himself comfortable and opened comm-channels with the others.

"Are you in, Sub-sergeant?" Chen asked.

"Tight as a bug," Mule said.

"It's about time we got started," the sergeant said.

It took some time, but finally Mule heard faint, metallic clangs. Those must be the locks that held the torpedo onto its rack releasing. Afterward came a tumbling motion, which told Mule the cables holding the Phoenix had detached. They were on their own now, adrift in space.

Because of what the briefing officer had told them, Mule a good idea of the game plan. *Slovakia* would detach almost all of its torpedoes and drones. Actually, it detached all the Phoenix torpedoes and kept several drones behind.

Several of the torpedoes would act as decoys. The mothership had carried extras in case some malfunctioned before the battle date. The idea was to drop off each torpedo and expel it farther away from the mothership in a lateral direction, using magnetic impulse. In layman's terms, *Slovakia* magnetically repelled each torpedo and drone away from it at a varying angle.

Once the mothership braked, the many torpedoes and drones would continue at the original velocity. They would all seemingly leap ahead of *Slovakia*, but they would do so without giving themselves away through fusion-burn signatures.

Those would come later, days later, when the torpedoes and drones approached Tyche. For now, the captain hoped to work his silent torpedoes and drones as close to Tyche's surface as he could.

Inside the torpedo, Mule took a deep breath and tried to control his shakes. That he had them at all was a surprise. He wanted to attack, wanted to kill. So why did he shake?

"I'm going to watch a movie," Chen said. "I suggest the rest of you try to relax."

I don't get this. Why am I shaking? The cyborgs had spotted *Slovakia* too far out. Maybe his subconscious mind was worried about that. Maybe it thought the pod would become his coffin. Did the posthypnotic conditioning in the others actually have a real use?

"How are you feeling, Sarge?" Mule asked.

"You know what?" Chen said. "I'm excited. Yeah, I'm anxious to rip some cyborgs heads off their torsos."

"You can hardly wait?"

"Yeah," Chen said. "It's like a game of Fist-Ball, a championship match. I'm ready. We're all ready. Are you ready, Mule?"

"I live for danger."

The others chuckled at his words.

"The cyborgs are probably pissing oil right now," Chen said. "We're the Space Marines. We're the best there is. We have the latest tech and we're full of *Quake*. If I could feel sorry for them freaks, I would. Instead, I'm going to enjoy shooting their eyes out. They shine orange, I hear. Did you ever hear that?"

"Yeah," Mule said. He thought about the cyborg who had stared at his wife and kids.

"The pupils are colored orange cause of the circuits in their skull," Chen said. "Thinking about that makes me want to puke. I hate them, Mule. I want to stomp them like the bugs they are."

"Good."

It went on like that for a long time. Eventually, Mule cut the link with Chen and the others, still pumping themselves up. He brought up the torpedo's outer cameras and watched the stars. They were alone in the night, headed for Tyche, waiting to blast out of the nosecone and begin the pod assault. He could hardly wait, and he found that the shakes had stopped.

-4-

Day 1094: Mule awoke with a shout as a klaxon rang in his ears.

"What's going on?" Chen asked through the comm-link.

Mule squeezed his eyes shut, and with delicate patience, he eased his right arm out of the battlesuit's sleeve. He managed to work his hand under the collar and use his index finger to rub his itchy eyes.

"Mule, do you hear me?"

"Loud and clear, Sarge," Mule said. "What's up?"

"Do you hear the klaxon?"

"Sure."

They'd been in the Phoenix for five days already. *Slovakia* had braked hard and expelled a lead-laced gel cloud in front of it. That screened the vessel from the torpedoes and likely, from the cyborgs—unless the melds had put secret drones far afield that looked from behind *Slovakia*. Sometime during the five days, the cyborg missiles had increased gravities, coming at the mothership faster, as their fusion tails streaked for many kilometers behind them.

"Here it is," Chen said through the comm, "I was looking for the switch." The klaxon stopped.

Easing his right arm back into the battlesuit's sleeve, Mule turned on his computer. He had a few talents other than strict mayhem. Before he became a Marine, even before his Martian secret service days, Mule had been a hacker.

He'd had three years to think about the mission, three years to crawl around the mothership, poking here and there. He'd hacked into the main computer and written new programs for his battlesuit, giving himself some tricky options. Now he brought up an unauthorized image on his HUD. From signals emitting from the torpedoes and drones, he built a holoimage of the overall situation.

The planetoid's edge showed, as did the many tiny blips approaching it. Tyche neared or they neared Tyche. It was the same difference.

"Our torpedo is going to brake soon," Chen said over the comm-link. "Are you boys ready?"

The others signaled yes.

"Mule, what about you?" Chen asked.

"Give me a minute."

"Did you hear that we're going to brake?"

"I got that," Mule said. "Now wait a sec."

"What aren't you telling me?"

Mule snapped orders to his suit computer. Something strange was going on out there. An Alliance drone—a tiny green blip on his HUD—blinked with a dull gray color. Then so did another drone.

"Speak to me, Mule. That's an order."

Mule cursed softly under his breath.

"What's happening?" Chen asked.

"The cyborgs are using—" Mule winced as another drone went inert. "The cyborgs are doing something to our forward drones. I wonder if they've hacked into the control software."

"How do you know what's going on?"

Mule told him about his self-written programs.

"You can see the big picture?" Chen asked, with wonder in his voice.

The green blinking drones—a swarm of them—burst into motive life. On Mule's HUD, they showed little flickering tails. This meant that in real time long blue fusion exhausts grew behind them as they began to accelerate.

Once again, their torpedo's klaxon began to blare.

"It's an emergency!" Chen shouted to the others. "Get set. We're going to move."

As Sergeant Chen finished his sentence, the Phoenix's engine ignited.

Mule watched his HUD. Instead of flying faster at Tyche or slowing down, their torpedo slewed "upward" as if heading toward the planetoid's North Pole.

"I don't think we're slowing down," Chen said.

Slowing down had been the operational plan. If the torpedo moved at its original velocity and fired the Marine pods like bullets, each fighter would hit the surface hard enough to obliterate the powered armor shells. They had to slow down first so they could make softer landings. Ergo, the Phoenix needed to brake. For combat purposes—at least usually—the later they slowed down the better. Braking used the engines, blasting at full power. The exhaust heat easily registered on enemy sensor systems, making them targets.

"We're not braking just yet," Mule said. He told them what he knew so far.

"So what's happening?" Chen asked.

Mule was fiddling with his computer, activating more of his custom software.

The burn didn't last long for the Phoenix. Before the engine shut off, the torpedo's main computer readjusted their flight path, aiming at their former destination point once more.

"Mule, what are you hiding from us?" Chen asked.

"I'm not hiding anything, I don't know myself yet. I'm trying to figure out why this happened. My guess is the cyborgs used an invisible projectile against the drones. Our torpedo moved to avoid any other invisible projectiles sent at us."

"Invisible?"

"Unseen by our side's optics," Mule said.

He figured the captain didn't want to use active radar just yet. Once the captain used the ship's radar, he lit up the mothership like a beacon. Yet if the cyborgs already knew where *Slovakia* was, why not use radar? Something else was going on that Mule didn't comprehend.

Ninety minutes later, the captain spoke to them. The old man spoke to all the Marines in the many torpedoes. He used a relayed broadcast, and he no doubt emitted it from a drone well away from the mothership.

Mule heard the message in his headphones in his helmet. They all must have.

"This is Captain Han of *Slovakia* speaking. Each of your torpedoes just made a slight course shift. The reason is simple. The cyborgs fired black-ice projectiles at our forward drones. We believed they used steel sabots to magnetically accelerate the projectiles with rail-guns, as that's how we do it. The melds must have done it behind a gel cloud. We observed explosions in the gel cloud two days ago, but until now had no idea what they were. Those explosions must have opened holes for the black-ice projectiles.

"Drones lead the assault for just such a reason," the captain said. "The cyborg projectiles hit several of our drones, smashing enough internal gear to render them inoperative. It means the cyborgs must have used optics to spot the majority of you after launch."

Mule could have already told him that, as it was obvious.

"I don't want you men to worry," the captain said. "The drones have already begun to accelerate at Tyche. Soon, your torpedoes will begin to brake."

The captain cleared his throat. "Gentlemen, it has been my pleasure to bring you this far. We haven't found any of these black-ice projectiles aimed at *Slovakia*, but we must presume that many are flying at us. Our gel cloud might deflect some of them enough to throw them off course, but the mothership is in danger nonetheless. Since each of your torpedoes must be on cyborg screens, the tactical AI has decided on a new Marine landing strategy."

Mule felt a surge of fear squeeze his spine. That didn't sound good.

There was a longer pause this time. "We had hoped to bring the Phoenixes nearer the planetoid before we had them brake," the captain said. "That's not going to happen now."

"Is he talking about a change in the battle plan?" one of the Marines asked.

"Shut up!" Chen snapped. "Listen to the captain."

"There is an emergency release code in each of your torpedoes," the captain was saying. "This mission, you will not launch through the firing tubes as planned, nor will you insert onto the planetoid in your pods. Instead, you will crawl out of the hatches you first entered. You will find emergency hoses inside the compartment and an escape hatch from the torpedo. Listen closely, gentlemen. This could be a tricky and unorthodox operation."

"Sir, tell them about the braking," an officer said over the comm-link. "They need to allow their craft to brake before they attempt any of this."

"I hope you men heard that," the captain said. "First, each torpedo will lower its velocity through a swift but intense braking schedule. That means you're going to be in space longer than we had anticipated. You may be alive and heading for Tyche even after *Slovakia* is—"

"Sir!" an officer interrupted.

"Gentlemen," the captain raised his voice to override his officer as he continued addressing the Marines. "You will attach the life-support and waste hoses to your battlesuits. Then you will use the escape hatch and uncoil the lines as far as they will go. That's a hundred meters in most cases, and for a few of you, it will be two hundred meters. You will float outside the torpedo in space."

"What?" Hayes asked. "That's crazy. We've never practiced for that."

Mule shook his head. Marine landing insertions were always in pods fired from torpedoes. It sounded as if they were going to free-fall their way down. The captain and his tac-team must be really worried to try a stunt like this.

"The next part of the journey is going to last several days longer than we'd first planned," the captain said. "The torpedo's AI will alert you once it is ready to accelerate at the planetoid. It will do that just before impact. You must detach before the torpedo accelerates its final time. The torpedo will proceed down to Tyche ahead of you and, we hope, destroy cyborg infrastructure. None of you is going to land in a pod, but rather through free-fall. Each of you will also have a higher insertion velocity than we had originally anticipated. The main AI suggests that the depth of the methane ice will sufficiently break your falls so…so most of you will survive a crash landing."

"Is he kidding?" Hayes muttered. "He must be kidding."

"Shut up!" Chen snarled.

"This is a desperate situation, gentlemen. We've always known the cyborgs were cunning. They love deception and stealth attacks above all else. But you are the Alliance Space Marines. You must land and destroy every cyborg, or destroy the life-support cubicles and the planetoid's motive power. You cannot let the cyborgs use Tyche for whatever evil purpose it has been modified to perform."

Several Marines growled agreement.

"I'm going offline soon," the captain said. "After I do, the tech advisor is going to switch to the command channel and speak to the sergeants. He has a few technical aspects about the mission you'll each need to know. I would wish you gentlemen luck, but I know you don't need it. You're the toughest fighting force in history. And you will kick these cyborgs to death. Do you hear me?"

The growls in Mule's ears grew in volume.

"Kill the cyborgs, Marines. Kill the cyborgs!"

***

Two hundred and nineteen minutes later, the Phoenix rotated so its engine port aimed at Tyche. The torpedo braked for seventy-eight minutes, reducing their velocity.

"The cyborgs are definitely going to see that," Chen said.

Mule didn't respond. He was too busy watching his HUD. *Slovakia* burst sideways through its own gel cloud, accelerating away from the enemy. The captain was playing by new rules. The black-ice projectiles had changed the game.

Mule shook his head. The new game meant the mothership was simply another decoy.

As *Slovakia* shut off its engine, a laser beam appeared from the ship. The laser speared toward Tyche at some distant target.

"We're rotating," Chen said.

The deceleration aboard the torpedo had quit. The torpedo must be aligning itself back on target.

The minutes ticked by, and *Slovakia's* laser stopped beaming. Mule wondered what the ship had been firing at. A new gel cloud began to form before it, sprayed from outer gel tanks. The mothership couldn't keep flying through its gel cloud and hope to have some sort of protection left later. None of that would matter, however, if the captain didn't stop the five missiles.

If the captain or the AI is smart, Mule thought, *he should put a gel cloud behind them, too.* Maybe the captain had already done that.

"It's time to move out," Chen said.

Mule unhooked his tubes, checked his suit and detached the buckles. He crawled and knocked on the hatch with an armored boot.

A Marine opened the hatch and helped him out.

"Open up your helmets," Chen told them.

Mule found the side control and pressed it. The visor eased open like a Cyclops' eye. Cold, metallic-tasting air seeped past his face and down his neck.

He peered at his squad-mates. Everyone had a heavy growth of beard.

Hayes had bloodshot eyes, and every time he glanced somewhere, the man's eyes rolled as if they were loose in his head.

"Are you feeling okay?" Mule asked him.

Hayes muttered a litany of profanities and described in detail what he was going to do with his fist to the cyborgs.

After Hayes finished speaking, Chen spoke for several minutes. Soon, he had everyone nodding.

They helped each other open the battlesuits and climb out.

Mule practiced isometric exercises. It felt good to be out of the suit and in the chamber's chilly air. Then he scratched everywhere. Others arm-wrestled or practiced zero-G moves on each other. Due to their open suits, the chamber smelled worse than a locker room.

Finally, they shook hands all around and slapped each other on the shoulders. One by one, they climbed back into their suits and checked each other's locks.

"Mule and I will use the two-hundred-meter hoses," Chen said.

Mule hooked up his hoses.

When everyone signaled they were ready, Chen pulled a lever and blew open the emergency hatch. Its metal plate flew off into space, tumbling end over end before disappearing into the distance. There came a momentary tug as the air rushed out. Mule didn't move, though, as he'd anchored himself with his magnetized boots.

Finally, the Marines demagnetized and jumped out of the hatch. They drifted to the ends of their lines, according to the new plan.

Before, the torpedo's battle computer would have figured out trajectories and a hundred other little problems for them. It would have launched them perfectly at the surface in their insertion pods. Now their velocity was low enough…maybe, to survive a free-fall landing on the ice. Now they were outside the torpedo so if the cyborgs destroyed the delivery vehicle, some of them might survive its destruction and land on the surface to wreak vengeance against the melds.

-5-

Day 1095: Space war had its own rules. It was a giant game of hide-and-seek. The stellar void was vast, making it nearly impossible to see a cold dark object, particularly if it was composed of radar-resistant material like black ice.

Hide from radar, hide from optic sight and keep one's thermal signature down to nothing if possible, those were key techniques. From the very beginning, the cyborgs possessed better sensors and better stealth material.

Humans liked protection, armor. Their best battleships had thick, asteroid-like particle shields, matter hundreds of meters thick. The genetically-engineered Highborn had developed collapsium armor of densely packed atoms. Here in the Oort cloud, ordinary humans possessed none of those advantages.

As Mule drifted in space, tethered to the Phoenix, he did some computing. Either the Neptunians when they'd been alive, or the cyborgs, had built a massive exhaust port onto Tyche. That implied vast, planetoid-sized engines. That in turn implied more than one or two Lurkers: more like twenty of the stealth vessels. If Tyche swarmed with melds, two thousand Marines wouldn't have much of a chance. In fact, if that were the reality—thousands of cyborgs—maybe the melds would attempt to capture rather than to kill them.

Capture would be worse than death. The cyborgs were a nightmare, but their leaders were worse. A Web-Mind was a cyborg times one thousand. Humanity had been fighting them long enough now to know the worst. The melds teased brain mass from involuntary donors, from prisoners of war. They spread out and wired the brains onto flats, inserted control circuitry into the tissues and submerged it all into computing gel, which they put into bio domes. The combined brain masses made the Web-Mind into a strange intellect with an inconceivable IQ.

If the cyborgs captured him and tore him down for his brain…would he live the rest of his days in soundless horror, part of a vast, living, pulsating Web-Mind?

Thinking about it enraged Mule. Maybe others would open their visor one last time and choke on nothing, on vacuum. He had a different plan. He was going to make the Web-Minds fear him. If he could, he would make it to one of the brain domes. Then he'd shoot the domes one by one, telling them about his wife, about his children and about Mars. Afterward, he'd watch the brains quiver in terror as those around them died one by one.

The minutes merged into hours, and Mule focused on the space battle going around him. It proved interesting for a while, watching through his illegal HUD feed.

The captain's next big move was a sudden and very powerful nuclear explosion in the path of the enemy missiles.

Almost by accident, Mule caught a bit of the info, the explosion. He switched the imaging on his HUD to get a better idea of what was going on. The five cyborg missiles zeroed in on the mothership—well, on the spreading gel cloud many hundreds of thousands of kilometers ahead of them. The missiles didn't bunch together, but came one at a time in a staggered formation.

After several seconds of scanning the situation, Mule understood what must have happened. Days ago, the captain must have used the mothership's sole rail-gun. Behind the gel cloud, he'd shot steel-skinned sabot rounds. The rail-gun accelerated the sabots and then the round shed its metallic skin. The inner kernels were polymer mines: dark, radar-resistant and optically difficult to detect. Each mine would have secretly burst through the gel cloud and continued to fly on an intercept pattern toward the approaching missiles, or rather, where the missiles would be at a projected intercept time.

As Mule scanned the data, he realized a proximity mine had just exploded—a powerful thermonuclear weapon. It created a mighty EMP near the approaching missiles.

Grinning so hard it made his mouth hurt, Mule ran analyses on the enemy missiles. According to the readings, the EMP had taken out three of them.

The last two missiles accelerated, closing in on the gel cloud.

A small explosion occurred in the lead-laced cloud. It was certainly a *Slovakia*-engineered event. The explosion punched a hole through the gels, creating a window, an opening. Through the window speared the mothership's lone laser. The beam washed the nosecone of the front missile, and seconds later, the cyborg warhead detonated.

Then came another small explosion in the gel cloud, creating a new window. The laser speared out of it. But it was too late. The last cyborg missile—a big thing one quarter the size of *Slovakia*—had already spewed a cloud of prismatic crystals.

Those crystals were a laser defensive layer. Each crystal reflected light. When a laser attempted to burn through—as *Slovakia's* beam tried now—each crystal stole and diffused some of the laser's strength. The beam turned crystals into slag-material and began devouring the sludge through heat. A burn-through took time, depending on a P-Cloud's thickness and the intensity of the laser.

Likely, Captain Han knew he didn't have the time because the prismatic cloud was too thick. The beam snapped off, and the cyborg missile continued boring in.

The critical event in the drama occurred soon thereafter. The cyborg missile entered the lead-laced cloud. As the missile did that, many hundreds of kilometers away, the mothership plowed out of the cloud, with its fusion engine engaged.

It told Mule the captain had been waiting for just that event. While hidden behind the cloud, Han must have maneuvered the mothership away from the enemy missile. Captain Han tried to pull a fast one.

The cyborg missile detonated. Mule didn't witness the thermonuclear explosion, but his computer could tell because of the reaction of the gel cloud. The lead lacing in the cloud helped dampen some of the blast and radiation, but not all and maybe not enough.

Several minutes later, Captain Han came online. "We survived, but many of us have taken deadly dosages of gamma rays. We're not sure how long we can last, but we'll put the mothership on autopilot in case we all succumb to the radiation."

The captain coughed. It sounded bad. He must have taken a heavy dosage, and if he had, how much had the rest of the bridge crew taken?

The Marine squad outside the torpedo continued on the collision course with the planetoid, now with a possibly dying mothership behind them. Tyche loomed before them. Out here in the Oort cloud, it was almost absolute zero, so cold that methane froze hard. The planetoid had a high albedo due to the surface ice.

As the remaining Alliance drones neared Tyche ahead of the torpedoes, the cyborgs must have detonated a proximity mine of their own. On his HUD, Mule witnessed a thermonuclear EMP. The blast took out most of the remaining drones. Three survived the explosion. Two of them were X-ray shooting missiles. These sprouted metal rods on their nosecones and detonated their own nuclear cores.

The gamma and X-rays advanced ahead of the blast destruction. Rods in the nosecone focused the rays at whatever the drone radar had discovered. Those gamma and X-rays beamed onto Tyche's surface. Fractions of a second later, the nuclear fireball destroyed the rods and the rest of the drone.

The final drone, a hardened missile, dove onto the surface and exploded just as it touched.

On his HUD, Mule saw a bloom of fire. The warhead exploded on the methane ice, causing vast crackling on the surface.

"The missiles are softening up the enemy for us!" Chen shouted.

Mule wanted to cheer. But instead he kept wondering about the best way to land in free-fall. How far should he bend his knees? It was too bad he didn't have a suit thruster. If he'd been in his pod and ejected from the torpedo as planned, he wouldn't have to worry about any of this. The free-fall landing changed the procedures.

After a half day more of travel time, the Marines finally neared Tyche, their comm chatter constant now. They used comm lasers directly toward each other so the cyborgs couldn't pick up the talk. Enemy black-ice projectiles hit the lead torpedoes, destroying many but sparing the men on the lines. Luckily, theirs was one of the last struck.

"Detach, detach, detach!" Chen shouted as they neared their target.

"That's not going to give us enough separation," Mule said.

"What are you talking about?"

"If we're only one hundred meters away from a destroyed torpedo, we'll still be in range of flying shrapnel from the impact explosion. If we hope to survive, we have to be farther away from our ride."

"Talk to me, Mule," Chen said. "Give me a suggestion."

Mule was already reeling himself down to the torpedo. "We have to reach the hull, detach the hoses and jump as hard as we can. We need distance from our torpedo and the jumping will give us that."

Through his headphones, Mule heard the roars of dying and outraged Marines ahead of him.

"You heard Mule," Chen told the others of their squad. "Let's hurry." The sergeant began contacting other torpedoes, telling them the same thing.

Mule hauled as fast as he could. How much time did they have? He saw his squad-mates reaching the torpedo. Detached hoses sprayed air and mist as the Marines let them go. Then, one after another, his fellow squad-mates jumped. Hayes and Sumo first magnetically walked to the downward side of the torpedo, and jumped in that direction.

Mule yanked on his hoses so he drifted down. He magnetized his boots and soon clanged against the hull. Chen landed nearby, having done the same thing.

"This is a crazy way to make a surface landing," Chen said.

"Love the Corps or get out," Mule said.

"Semper fi," Chen said.

Mule leaped. Chen leaped, too. Their detached hoses flapped and twisted like snakes.

Tyche loomed huge before them, getting bigger by the minute.

"Look at it!" Hayes said.

Mule looked down in time to see the torpedo's nosecone crumple. Something ripped it open. Then the Phoenix began to tumble, spinning faster as it approached the planetoid.

"We wouldn't have survived that," Chen said. "You saved our lives, Mule."

The others sent him thanks too.

The minutes ticked down, and there were more shouts on the headphones, more dying Marines.

"Sand!" a Marine sergeant shouted over the comm. "The cyborgs are shooting high velocity clouds of sand at us. It's ripping through seams and breaking faceplates."

"Position yourselves feet-first at the planet," Mule said. "Use your cameras to angle it right and run a gyro program on your computers to help keep you on target."

He did exactly as he suggested, and he used guide-jets to help position himself. Tyche filled his world, his camera vision. He saw lights on the surface and something bloomed into existence. Was that a nuclear fireball? Was it a sand-cannon blasting at them?

Minutes went by. He heard something odd then, and he felt waves of pressure against the bottom of his feet.

What the—

Mule realized it must be sand, varying thicknesses of it.

Sumo bought it because he tilted his head forward and took it right in the faceplate, a big gust without realizing it. Granules cracked his visor and vacuum did the rest.

"We're down to four," Chen said.

Marine chatter grew continuous. Men swore savagely at the cyborgs and promised direst vengeance.

"Just let us get down!" a sergeant roared. "We're Marines, and we're here to kick your guts straight through to your butts, you metal heads!"

Mule worked his guide-jets, trying to align himself perfectly and to keep himself that way. How many on their side

34

had survived so far? How many Marines would survive planetfall? The mothership had launched two thousand men.

Although Mule checked his space program HUD, he failed to spot any igniting engines. It seemed the cyborgs had destroyed all the torpedoes. By the comm chatter, Mule figured there must be one third of the men left. Maybe there were six hundred and fifty Marines to conquer this last planetoid. Probably it was even less, maybe four hundred or three hundred and fifty Marines.

Tyche in his vision grew until it blocked all the stars. Now Mule plunged down toward the planet.

"I'm going to kill you cyborgs!" Chen roared. "I'm going rip off your heads and piss down your necks!"

"Concentrate on landing," Mule reminded him.

"What?"

"You have to land intact before you can kill anyone."

"Right," Chen said. "Yeah, that's good advice. Hey, you goons, this is it. You'd better land straight on your feet and get the servos ready. If any of you apes fails me now I'm going make you wish you were dead."

"We will be dead then, Sarge," Hayes said.

"Just do what I say, and no back talk."

"Sure, Sarge," Hayes said.

Mule concentrated, and he wondered if this was going to break his legs.

"Luck, Marine," Chen said.

Mule nodded. He was through talking. The surface rushed at him, and concern beat though him like a heartbeat. He found himself breathing harshly. The icy methane rushed nearer and nearer.

Mule roared, and he bent slightly at the knees. Would his servos hold? Was the captain still alive or was *Slovakia* a drifting ghost ship in the Oort cloud? He didn't have any more time to wonder. The icy surface rushed up, and Mule slammed against it.

It felt as if the soles of his feet were shoved up against his chin. Servos whined. Battlesuit metal screeched and he heard blasting noises and crackling ice.

No. That didn't make sense. Vacuum couldn't carry noise. Maybe the ice touching his suit could. Wait a minute…this little planetoid had a negligible atmosphere, a touch of nitrogen. Could that carry the sound?

Mule plunged through the methane ice. It was a white blur on his HUD. The suit servos whined, and he felt himself slowing, slower and then he came to a stop. He blinked several times, breathing deeply. He had stopped moving. He had landed. He was alive.

He almost opened communications with Chen. Caution stilled the impulse. He didn't want the cyborgs to triangulate open communications and pinpoint their locations.

Mule swallowed a lump down his throat. First flexing his fingers, he thrust his metal-protected hands into the ice and began to climb out of the gopher-like hole his plunge down from space had made. It was time to find the others and decide on their nearest objective.

-6-

Day 1096: Mule found Sergeant Chen first. The Marine's landing into the ice had sent out jagged lines of crackling methane around the hole. The sergeant pushed his head and shoulders out of the impact-created tunnel, staring up at Mule with his black faceplate, watching him.

A moment later, Chen climbed onto the surface. The gorilla in his battlesuit looked around at the bleak world. Afterward, Chen clumped beside Mule and turned on the link-line between their two suits. It was extremely short-range communication, meaning they could talk without any cyborgs listening in.

"Did you find any of the others?" Chen asked.

"Not yet."

"We got to start looking."

Mule scanned the barren icescape with his sensors. The visor gathered ambient starlight and gave him a simulated HUD. Tyche's surface wasn't smooth, but had ripples in it. That implied something in times past had made the methane into sludge or liquid so it could freeze in this manner. Did Tyche have cryovolcanoes as Triton did?

Several minutes later, Mule spotted another of their squad climbing out of a hole with the obligatory crack lines spreading outward. It was Hayes. He lived, although one of his left leg servos sparked. Hayes told them he could hear it whine.

"That can't be good," Hayes added over the link-line.

Silently, Mule agreed. Marines needed mobility in order to employ their best tactics, and that went quadruple against cyborgs. If the servo gave out or limited Hayes's mobility—this Hell-world would devour any mistakes or missteps.

Ten minutes later, Mule spotted the last hole. Like theirs, the tunnel slanted and didn't go straight down. He shined a light down the hole but couldn't see anything moving. He was the scout, so he crawled into the tunnel and found a dead Marine at the bottom. It was Red, and his neck was broken. Mule took what he could off the battlesuit. Unfortunately, he would have needed a machine shop to pry off Red's servos and put a good one into Hayes's injured suit.

We made it, or three of us did. I wonder how many other Marines are down.

At the moment, they had three fighters, four gyroc rifles, one plasma flamer and many extra APEX rounds. What they didn't have was an endless air supply.

"We need to find the cyborgs pronto," Chen said. "They breathe air, don't they?"

"Last I heard," Mule said.

"Which way do we go, sniper?"

Mule ran another program and slowly turned in a circle. He raised an arm. "That way; we head in Tyche's north."

"What are you reading?"

"Oxygen traces."

"Let's get moving," Chen said. "We need to get near the oxygen traces and fix our location of attack. What do you say, sniper? Do we move together or are you going to see what's there first?"

That was a good question. Mule gave it several seconds thought. "Let's stick together for now. We need to find others before we do any attacking."

"Hey," Hayes said, "I'm picking up a voice. It's weak, though."

"What direction?" Chen asked.

"Behind us," Hayes said, "that way." The gorilla with the sparking left knee-joint raised an arm and pointed.

"I think you're right," Chen told Mule. "We need numbers and firepower before we hit the cyborgs."

Mule grunted, and they headed across the barren world to see if other Marines had made it alive onto the surface.

***

Two hours and five more Marines later, the icescape had turned surreal with cracks or vents in the ice. Some of the vents billowed nitrogen and methane vapor a kilometer or more into the air. Occasionally vents spurted nitrogen or methane liquid. What a crazy place this was out here at the end of nowhere. *Welcome to the Oort cloud*, Mule thought.

The vents and vapors told Mule that Tyche had a heat source somewhere within the planetoid. The extent of the cryogeysers meant it had to be a greater source than mere radioactive decay. Could Tyche have a molten core like Earth? That seemed preposterous. Before its destruction, Triton in the Neptune gravitational system had been heated by friction, the tidal forces that pulled and pushed the moon as it orbited the gas giant. There couldn't be any tidal forces out here because there was no gravity source to cause them.

What had the Neptunian scientists been doing out here anyway? They had been capitalists, meaning that something like a distant Oort Cloud science station would have needed to turn a profit sooner rather than later. Was there something more to Tyche that they didn't know about?

Mule spied a distant flicker of motion. He used extreme magnification. "Get down," he shouted, "and don't move!"

He sprawled onto on the ice, hoping his chameleon systems hid him from the enemy. The others did likewise, big men in heavy battlesuits trying to blend in.

"What's wrong?" Chen asked through the link-line.

"Check HUD three-nine-nine," Mule whispered. "Use extreme magnification."

"What *is* that?" Chen asked. "It can't be indigenous life, but it is moving."

In Mule's opinion, the unknown contact was flying above the surface, just above the ice, maybe by a few meters.

"Okay," he said, scanning the computer analysis on his HUD. "I'm picking up some readings. It's metallic and hot."

"Radioactive?" Chen asked.

"No—*hot*, heat exhaust," Mule said.

"The cyborgs have a skimmer?"

"Whatever you want to call it," Mule said. "Skimmer sounds good."

"They're headed here?" Chen asked.

"Yup."

Sergeant Chen rolled onto his back so he stared up at the stars. He held the position for a short time until he faced the approaching enemy again.

"Listen close," Chen said. "We're splitting up into two-man teams so they can't kill us with a single missile or skimmer cannon, laser, whatever that thing has, and we have to try to ambush it. If you're out of link-line range, maintain comm silence. Try to use the cryogeysers for cover. Mule, you're coming with me. Hayes, I'll carry the flamer for now."

Soon, Chen and Mule loped across the ice, staying close together. They used low-gravity jumps, almost an extended glide, to cover ground fast. Mule's boots crunched against ice each time he landed to take another bound.

"They're sure to see us," Mule said.

"I'm counting on the melds having motion detectors," Chen said.

"That's means we're making ourselves bait."

"Never ask your men to do something you're not willing to do yourself," Chen said. "This looks like a good spot. Get down and set up your rifle."

They landed behind an icy protrusion that was layered like a smooth wedding cake. It told Mule this must have come from a cryovolcano that had spewed liquid methane.

"What makes this planetoid so hot?" Mule asked.

"Concentrate, Marine. It's firefight time."

Mule watched the distant object. It had gotten larger-looking and was moving faster than he'd realized. He readied his gyroc rifle. The APEX rounds could take down a cyborg in body armor. It should be able to punch through the hull of a skimmer.

Time dragged as he waited. Cryogeysers continued to blow vapor, although it wasn't continuous. He looked around. The four fire-teams had gone to ground and the skimmer loomed larger yet.

"Too bad we don't have heavy lasers," Mule said.

"Does the skimmer have a canopy, an enclosed compartment?" Chen asked.

"No. It's an open-air craft."

"Can you count the occupants?" Chen asked.

"Crap!" Mule shouted. "They're firing missiles."

A streak pulled away from the skimmer and moved above the ice. It split in two. No, no, there must have been two missiles to begin with. One zeroed in on them. The other missile presumably headed for another team.

"Keep your rifle aimed at the skimmer," Chen said. The sergeant lay behind the tripod flamer. With a flip of his gloved finger, he activated the heavy weapon.

"It must be a homing missile," Mule said. "They've locked onto our signatures. Should we split up to confuse it?'"

"I said sit tight," Chen snarled, "and shut up. Let me concentrate."

Mule licked his lips. The skimmer kept coming, but the two missiles came faster. They were sleek things, only a little bigger than a Marine in his battlesuit. Like Earth-side cruise missiles, they skimmed just over the surface, minutely changing course as they zeroed in on their target.

"Here it comes!" Mule shouted.

As if he was on the firing range, Sergeant Chen pressed the flamer button. For a second, Mule knew it was hopeless. Landing impact must have jarred something loose in the flamer. The superheated plasma weapon took careful calibrations to work right, and—

An orange globule of plasma discharged from the flamer. The superheated substance actually seemed to wobble as it flew into the dark atmosphere. The plasma expanded as it traveled, and the missile plowed into the superheated orange glow.

"Shove yourself against the ice!" Chen shouted.

Mule had already thrown himself onto the ground. The missile explosion clicked on his sensors. The practically nonexistent atmosphere wasn't dense enough to carry the sound or the blast waves of the explosion powerfully enough to affect them.

Mule breathed a sigh of relief. The warhead was explosive but not nuclear. He breathed two more times and figured his suit was intact, without breaches.

He lifted his head and realigned the rifle. The skimmer was closer.

"They're launching another one," Mule said.

The missile dropped from the undercarriage and streaked ahead of the skimmer. The missile had their names written on it, as it zoomed straight at their position.

Chen swore as the flamer began to recharge. It only had seven charges left, but none of those would build up fast enough to help them.

"Let's split up," Chen said.

"But the missile will just follow—"

"Do as I tell you!" Chen roared. He activated the flamer and took a flying leap away to the left, leaving the flamer behind.

Mule scrambled to his feet and bounded with low-gravity leaps to his right. He clutched his rifle, and he expected to see the missile swerve to track him or Chen. Either way, he would miss the Sarge—

The missile slammed against the heat-building flamer where it sat alone on the ice, exploding. Mule saw it through his HUD using his rearward-aimed sensors.

Right, right, the sergeant had activated the flamer, making it hot. The missile must have homed in on it.

More explosions occurred beside vaporous geyser vents. The explosions came from other, striking missiles. How many did the skimmer carry?

Mule raised his rifle, and he snapped off five shots, quick firing at the approaching skimmer. The armor-piercing explosive rounds were smart. They wouldn't swerve around corners, but like the missiles a moment ago, they could make course corrections.

Were the other Marines firing? He hoped so. Mule took one more shot, jumped away and skidded across the ice on his belly, sliding for a hundred meters and behind another icy protrusion.

"Yeah!" a Marine shouted over the comm. It sounded like Hayes.

Mule swiveled on his torso and climbed up the ice wall. He cranked up the magnification to get a better look. The open-car skimmer had bullet holes and crumpled metal in the main body. Sparks showered in places. The skimmer wobbled from side to side and something red blew up inside it. Mule grinned. Gyrocs had hit all right.

Three cyborgs appeared in the cockpit. Two leaped overboard, one on either side of the craft. The last tried to bail out of the back, but didn't move fast enough. Before it got out, the skimmer nose-dived and plowed into ice. That crumpled the square-like body and sent showers of icy shards into the air. There wasn't a last movie explosion devouring the vehicle, but that thing looked wrecked.

The cyborg that went down with the skimmer survived the impact. Those bastards were hard to kill.

The meld stood slowly amidst the wreckage. It must be shaken up. That was something, at least. They didn't die easily, but it was possible to make one woozy. Before Mule could think about it too much, his gyroc rounds slammed into its body-armor, causing the cyborg to jerk and sway like a puppet. After that, the thing actually brought up a weapon. Mule could see severed power cables glowing orange inside its shattered body and yet still it attempted to fight. Then more of his rounds smashed its head, killing the thing as it slammed down against the wreckage.

"Communications silence isn't going to help us now," Chen said over the open comm-channel. "Count off and see how many of us are left."

They had Hayes, Chen, Ross and Mule, half of the eight who had begun the firefight with the skimmer. The cyborg missiles had borne bitter fruit. Now four Marines had to face off against two cyborgs—except a piece of luck finally touched their side. Because Chen used the open comm, three other Marines answered.

"This is Sub-sergeant Bogdan of Omega Squad. Give me your position."

Chen told him.

"We're five kilometers away," Bogdan said.

"Listen up, Marines," Chen said. "We're falling back to buy time until Bogdan gets here. But you'd better hurry, Sub-sergeant, or we won't be alive."

"We're coming as fast as we can," Bogdan said.

Mule didn't think pulling back was a good idea because exposing himself to cyborgs sounded foolish. He stayed where he was, and he clicked on a private comm-line to Chen. Before he could say anything, Mule saw two pulse lasers wash Ross's battlesuit as the Marine tried to jump away.

Ross landed, with his feet slipping out from under him. Was he in pain? He scrambled back onto his feet and leaped again, avoided another pulse and rolled into an ice crevice where vented vapors billowed.

"I'm hit," Ross said. "I'm leaking air."

"That's bad luck," Mule whispered. Without air—

"I'm sorry to hear that, Space Marine," Chen said. "You've just volunteered to be the decoy. I wish it could be some other way, but now you have to get up and jump again. We'll fix their positions and avenge you."

Mule knew Chen was right. If Ross leaked air, he wouldn't last long. In fact, the oxygen leak would make him easy to spot.

Ross spoke up. "Semper fi, Marines, you apes remember me." He leaped out of the crevice, sailing high toward the cyborgs. It was a good idea. They would have been expecting a low, gliding leap, not a high parabolic jump.

From up there in the atmosphere, Ross told them. "I see one." The Marine got off a shot. Then heavy pulses hit him, lighting him up. Something sizzled in the battlesuit. Ross roared in pain, got off a second gyroc shot and then cyborg laser pulses caused the Earther to gurgle as he choked on his own blood.

Mule lay on his torso and zeroed in on an enemy location. He snapped off three rounds. The rocket motors burned brightly as they flew at the enemy. The penetrators hit ice, but no cyborgs. The melds were fast. They fired and scooted each time, never staying still.

"I hate these things," Hayes snarled.

"Mule, look to your left," Chen shouted.

Mule swiveled, and rolled. A laser pulse struck the ice beside him, sending up methane vapor. He jumped low so his battlesuit headed toward a depression that would hide him from cyborg view. Another pulse came. The laser bolt skimmed ice and caught the edge of his suit just as he rolled into the crevice.

Heat washed against Mule's right leg. It felt like needles stabbing into his thigh. The suit's air-conditioning unit hummed, trying to cool him.

Hayes leaped toward a new position, twisted, fired and yelled "Sarge," and received two direct hits, two more and a final finishing shot that must have burnt his circuitry and probably his liver and other organs. Methane vapors hid his battlesuit as the heated metal landed and sank into the ice.

Meanwhile, Mule was low-gravity gliding. He was good at this.

"Get down," Chen said. "You're in the direct line of fire."

Mule barely reached an outcropping of protection. Pulses struck at precisely that moment. One missed. The other hit, washing him with heat.

Inside the battlesuit, blisters appeared on Mule's back. The lasers heated up his armor so there was a fused spot. The pain knocked the breath out of him. For a second, Mule expected the worst, a suit breach. It didn't happen, but his rear sensors burned out. There would be no looking back now with HUD imaging unless he turned his head toward what he wanted to see.

"I hit one," Chen said. "It's still moving, but I slowed it down. They were concentrating on you."

Mule found himself short of breath and thirsty like he couldn't believe. He refused to gulp water, though. He didn't know how long his battlesuit supply was supposed to last. He would sip later once he regained clear thinking and could ration his drinks, his precious water supply.

The hurt cyborg kept popping up, firing at Chen and then at Mule. They used their gyroc rounds against it and even blasted through the ice to try to finish the sneaky thing. Even hurt, the meld was too good for that, too fast and clever for their smart rounds. What the cyborg did, however, was fix their attention on it.

"It's baiting us," Mule said.

"What?" Chen asked. "Where's the undamaged meld?"

"Behind you!" one of Bogdan's three reinforcing Marines said.

Mule whirled around and a touch of envy and admiration filled him. The cyborg leaped faster and lower than he would ever be able to. The thing fired at him from a distance, and the round would have hit if Mule hadn't received the second of warning. He dropped into a crevice, a ready-made trench.

"It's between us," Chen said. "We'll cut it to ribbons now."

The sergeant was wrong. The cyborg was fast and wickedly clever. It took out two of the new Marines before one of Mule's APEX rounds knocked it off its feet.

"Shoot it!" Chen roared. "Kill it before it gets back up."

They were almost too slow. Three Marines on their bellies, from three different points on the compass fired in unison and only one round hit the meld. Fortunately, that shot proved vital, knocking the cyborg down again, this time to its stomach.

Mule stood up in his trench and fired three APEX shells. He saw the rocket contrails in the darkness. The super-hardened penetrators pierced the meld's body armor and killed it finally, for good.

"Where's the injured cyborg?" Mule asked.

They scanned the dark icescape, but found no sign of it.

"That can't be good," Bogdan said.

There were three of them, three Marines out of eleven. For the heavy cost of eight dead, they'd managed to destroy two cyborgs.

"Let's check the skimmer," Chen said. "Maybe we can use something on it."

"Are you kidding?" Mule said. "We have to find the cyborg before we try to salvage anything."

"Are you frightened, Martian?" Bogdan asked. Bogdan and Mule had never gotten along.

"Yeah, I'm quivering," Mule said.

"Listen, scrub—"

"Stow it," Chen said. "We're Marines. We stick together in the face of the enemy."

Bogdan remained silent. So did Mule.

The three of them neared until they were fifty meters from each other. Slowly, warily, keeping an eye out for the other cyborg—

"It's by the skimmer," Mule said. "Do you see it? The thing is crawling to the vehicle."

Mule raised his rifle and fired several shells. One slammed into the cyborg, but it managed to reach the skimmer nonetheless. There, the cyborg must have done something, because the remains of the skimmer exploded, sending wreckage and presumably cyborg body parts into the air.

"There's your dangerous meld," Bogdan sneered. "It was so frightened it suicided on us."

"Let's get link-lined," Mule said. "We're not under combat conditions anymore and shouldn't give ourselves away any more than we have too."

Chen kept his faceplate aimed at the destroyed skimmer and the suicidal meld. Finally, he faced them, and nodded.

Does Bogdan even realize the cyborg screwed us? Mule decided not to worry about it. As long as the sub-sergeant kept his gun aimed at the cyborgs, that's all that mattered.

-7-

The three Marines moved through the surreal icescape. It was dark, and geyser vents blew more frequently. A vaporous fog thicker than the negligible atmosphere drifted in places. Elsewhere, explosions and blooms of light appeared. Other Marines fought in the distance, some over one hundred kilometers away. There were snatches of words at times on open comm-channels. Then the voices went offline.

Mule studied some nearby vapors. What made the substance hot enough to spew? He had become more curious about that, not less.

"Do you still read the oxygen signatures?" Chen asked Mule through the link-line.

"Sure do, Sarge."

"How far away are they?"

"Another eleven kilometers," Mule said.

"We should speed up," Bogdan suggested.

"The cyborgs must have motion sensors near anything important," Mule replied. "Speeding up is a bad idea."

Bogdan turned toward him. Before the sub-sergeant could comment, a strangely emotionless voice spoke through their headphones.

"Your mission is futile."

"What?" Chen asked. "Mule, did you say that?"

"No."

"Well I didn't say it," Bogdan replied. "So it must have been the Martian."

The three of them spoke through the link-lines, staying off any comm-channel.

The emotionless voice spoke again. "I have come to understand that each of you was forced into attacking us. It is pitiful to consider the effort you've taken arriving here in the Oort cloud. It is pitiful because your mission is beyond useless."

"Who is that?" Chen asked. "Who do you think is speaking to us?"

"I think it's a cyborg," Mule said.

"What?"

"I just used my analyzer," Mule said. "The voice is synthetic."

"Circle up!" Chen shouted.

They did, Mule lifting his rifle and scanning the geyser-spewing terrain. "I don't see anything near," he said. "I'm going to extreme magnification."

"Good idea," Chen said. "I'm doing the same thing."

As they scanned while back-to-back, they slowly swiveled their helmeted heads.

"I don't see anything unusual," Bogdan said.

Chen grunted agreement, adding, "Where are they? I don't see them anywhere."

"Maybe the cyborg doesn't see us either," Mule said. "Maybe this is an open broadcast."

"So why would cyborgs start talking to their enemies?"

"Maybe it's trying to get inside our heads," Mule said. "Or it could be trying to get us to talk."

"I ain't afraid of them," Bogdan said.

"Stay off the comm," Chen said.

"I got that," Bogdan said. "I'm just saying I ain't afraid of it."

Mule continued searching. He examined the dirty ice. Did it have particles of dust in it, dirt, what? He scanned upward in case the melds used more skimmers or a space object near Tyche.

Obscured slightly by the faint nitrogen atmosphere and the occasional vapors from the geysers, some of the stars twinkled. The sight was so unexpected and shocking that it put an ache of homesickness in Mule's heart. He'd seen stars twinkle on Mars and later on Earth.

"The vast majority of your fellow Marines died in the futile attack," the emotionless voice told them. "I have already captured eighteen of your survivors. Three have decided to cooperate with me and talk."

"The thing's a filthy liar," Bogdan hissed.

"It's trying to work us," Mule said. "It's trying to get you angry so you do something stupid."

Bogdan turned toward him. "Listen to me, scrub."

"Shut up, Sub-sergeant," Chen said.

"Me?" Bogdan asked. "Look, the Martian's—"

"You will obey orders," Chen said, loudly.

Bogdan took his time answering. Finally, he nodded his helmet.

"Sub-sergeant," Chen said, "do you think the cyborg knows we're here, our exact location?"

Mule had been wondering about that. "Wait a minute…it said 'I' before. That implies individuality. Cyborgs are hive creatures. This is definitely an 'it' talking to us. It must be a Web-Mind."

"It's a *freak*," Bogdan muttered, with loathing.

"If you haven't already," the emotionless voice told them, "turn on your video sensors and observe the situation."

Mule hesitated. Why was a Web-Mind speaking to them? It wasn't for any good reason. The thing had a plan to screw them. Did it think they were stupid enough to talk with it so the creature could pinpoint their location?

Curiosity overcame Mule's caution. He thrust his chin against a sense-pad in his helmet, and he observed the video broadcast on his HUD.

He saw a naked, straining, powerfully muscled man strapped to a chair. The sight put a chill in Mule's heart. Cyborgs stood around the man. Computer panels and bio-equipment showed against a wall.

"That's Scar," Bogdan whispered in horror.

Mule recognized the man's pitted features. This wasn't just a vain boast then. Cyborgs had already captured Marines. His stomach twisted with revulsion. What were they doing to Scar? Why had they stripped him naked?

Mule switched his scrutiny from Scar to the cyborgs. The melds had human faces, each different to prove the things came from various people. But each cyborg wore its face like a mask in a lifeless, robotic manner. The eyes were so obviously artificial and the teeth silvery titanium that they were like demons with strange metal bodies. Some of the lights on the wall shined against their integral armor, reflecting brightly.

Scar struggled, with his big muscles bulging, but there was no working free for him. Sweat slicked his skin. Scar had his faults. The man also used to have a wife in England Sector. She'd died during the war. Scar had missed her badly.

Perhaps realizing this was the end, Scar looked up and roared at the cyborgs. Mule couldn't hear any words or sound. He just saw the corporal's horror, and it made Mule think of his wife and children.

Bogdan kept cursing, smacking his gloves hands together. Mule wouldn't be surprised if Bogdan went insane with fury and did something utterly rash.

On the HUD, a cyborg stretched out a metallic arm before Scar, showing the man a long steel needle with a weird, greenish-yellow solution with golden flecks floating in it. Scar shook his head. If a human had shown his captive a needle like that, there would have been gloating in the man's face. The cyborg's features showed nothing, which made the gesture even more chilling.

The cyborg plunged the needle into Scar's thick neck, squeezing the solution into the man. The Marine stiffened and he began to thrash, and he bellowed anew at the cyborgs, spraying salvia as he shouted silently. It didn't matter. The three cyborgs waited like traffic lights for the drug to take effect.

Soon, sound was added to Mule's video feed. It startled him. Then an unseen, emotionless speaker asked the corporal questions about the combat mission. Slack-faced now and slump-shouldered, Scar answered the questions one after another in a dull monotone.

"We came aboard the mothership *Slovakia*," Scar said in a slur, with salvia drooling from his mouth.

"The bastards," Bogdan whispered.

Mule closed his eyes. This was just so wrong. The Web-Mind had dehumanized Scar. The entire concept of cyborgs was dehumanizing to a frightful degree. How could people do this to each other? What was wrong with the human race that would allow some to create cyborgs?

Feeling as if he'd run forever, Mule opened his eyes and he continued to watch and listen.

"Tell me about hate-conditioning," the hidden speaker said.

In a halting manner, Scar did so. Occasionally, it appeared as if intelligence flickered in the corporal's eyes. He tried to stop speaking then, and agony of the soul welled within his orbs. Soon, thankfully, the eyes dulled again to the automaton the drug had made him.

"This is interesting, Marines," the emotionless speaker said. "Your masters have programmed you just as I do to my cyborgs."

Mule knew then that this was a Web-Mind speaking to them, one of the alien multi-minds. He hated it with desperate loathing.

"Your masters think of you as pawns, just as I think of my soldier units. Observe, please, your coming fate."

Two cyborgs dragged Scar to a table. They thrust him onto it and cinched straps into place. They put his head onto a skull-shaped cavity in the table. Saws levered down near his skull and began to whirl. One saw touched skull-bone and carefully cut and worked it open to expose his brain.

"No," Bogdan said. "They can't do this."

"Sarge," Mule said, "we can't watch this. The Web-Mind is trying to—"

"You metal freaks!" a Marine roared on an open line.

"Who is that?" Chen asked. "Who spoke? The idiot is using open communications."

For a second, Mule thought it was Bogdan. Then he realized the voice was wrong. "It must be someone from a different combat group."

"We know where you are!" the Marine shouted. "We're coming to get you!"

Mule flicked off the video and scanned the horizon. He saw it almost right away: an orange contrail highlighting a missile. This one was bigger than those fired from the skimmer earlier.

"Look," Mule said through the link-line. "The Web-Mind is responding to the boast. We were right. It must have done this to engage the hate-conditioning."

The missile was an easy twenty kilometers to their left. It rose higher and ignited into a nuclear fireball. Static hit the ether and the Marine yelling at the video cyborgs no longer broadcast his threats. Likely he and his group were dead. Scratch yet more Marines.

The three of them hit the ice and crawled behind rocky protrusions.

"What the heck is happening?" Chen asked. "Has everyone gone crazy?"

"Sarge," Mule said. "The Web-Mind figured out our weakness."

"What's that?"

"The hate-conditioning."

"Do you have any idea where the missile came from?" Bogdan asked Mule.

The shock of Scar's death seemed to have changed the sub-sergeant. "Sure," Mule said, "it came from where we're headed, about eleven kilometers away. At least the missile tells us we're headed toward the right place."

"The way I see it," Chen said, "the cyborgs figured out—"

"The Web-Mind did this," Mule said. "The Web-Mind runs the cyborgs. It's the devil we have to destroy."

"Agreed," Bogdan said.

"You're right, Mule," Chen said. There was iron in his voice. "The nuke shows the Web-Mind must have decided on trickery because it's afraid of us."

"It'd better be afraid," Bogdan whispered.

"Listen, you've both seen what's in store for us if they capture us," Chen said. "There's no going back, just forward. We don't even know whether our ship is still up there. Okay.

That's life. But for what those freaks did to our brothers, I say we make them pay ten thousand times."

"Make them pay," Bogdan said.

They couldn't make the cyborgs pay, but Mule didn't tell them that. There was only one creature they could make pay, and that was the Web-Mind.

"Let's go," Mule said.

***

Mule decided the Web-Mind didn't have long-range motion sensors, because if it did, it would have already been over for them. The Web-Mind must have used its horror tactic because some of *Slovakia's* missiles must have hit nerve centers.

Mule thought back to what he remembered about the original attack. One missile had hit the surface and another two had blasted vital areas—hopefully—with hard gamma and X-rays.

With their powered armor, the three Marines leaped low and long like Olympic broad jumpers. If they jumped too high, they would be a while coming down again. It wasn't like maneuvering on an asteroid, which could get tricky. Mule was better at this than the others were because he was a Martian, used to lower gravity.

The image of the needle stabbing Scar…Mule yearned to kill the Web-Mind and destroy every cyborg here. Had the melds done that to his wife, to his kids? The idea pulsed in his mind, creating rage. He worked to harness the anger. He would get vengeance, but he would use his head and use every tactic he could to win. If they solely replied on their emotions and charged ahead like the nuked Marines had done—

With an effort of will, he wrenched his thoughts onto a new track. He couldn't keep thinking about his lost wife and children. He needed to concentrate, to think.

If the cyborgs had slipped a Lurker out here, what did that mean? Movement to the Oort cloud was a big commitment for the cyborgs, just like it was for the Alliance. Lurkers were stealth troopships. How many Lurkers could the cyborgs have moved without anyone detecting them?

That was the first problem.

The second problem was different. Was Tyche an attack platform against the sunbeam, or was it the getaway vehicle to a new star system? If it was the attack platform, it seemed clear more cyborgs would have to join up later. Once Tyche neared the planets, the last cyborg spaceships would probably emerge to fight with it. But if the melds meant to slip away from the Solar System, wouldn't they need DNA to grow or clone more humans in order to harvest brains, eyes and spines? They would need advanced tech and enough of it to create a machine society in the new star system. Each of those items took cargo space in the Lurkers used to reach here.

He wondered about Lurkers and cargo spaces because of the Web-Mind's action of tormenting a prisoner to make Marines belligerent. It wasn't a common cyborg tactic.

More blooms appeared far in the distance. Were those yet more nuclear explosions? It told him other Marines still fought the cyborgs. The battle continued to rage as each group attempted to complete its tactical mission.

As Mule watched for more bloom or signs of battle, he noticed a cryovolcano. First vapor billowed out of a low hill or volcano. Then semi-liquid methane gushed out of the vent together with chunks of ice. The flow slid across the surface, expanding and radiating methane vapors. On Earth, the substance would have been scalding lava. Here, the substance was heated relative to the intensely cold planetoid. There were also cryogeyser vents nearby. The number had been increasing as they advanced on the cyborg structures.

Some of the vapor condensed higher up and drizzled down, creating a methane fog.

The cryovolcano sparked Mule's thoughts, particularly about Neptunians. Once, they had been the Solar System's premier capitalists.

Mule waved his arms until Bogdan and Chen noticed. They landed and turned around. He pointed at the bubbling cryovolcano until Chen nodded.

Mule jumped toward the vent until he landed a hundred meters from it. Some of the semi-liquid methane had already begun to harden into ice. He walked over and through that, cracking methane. As he neared the opening, he witnessed the sludge oozing past his legs. It resembled lava on Earth, except this stuff was cold to him, not hot. He dubbed it "cryomagma" in his own mind.

Wading ankle and then calf deep, he made it to the vent and peered at the cryomagma. It was slushy, icy sludge. How far did that stuff go down?

Thoughtfully, he jumped back to the others. They had moved closer to the cryovolcano. Each of them now used the link-line.

"What are you doing?" Chen asked.

"Have you noticed the geysers?" Mule asked.

"What about them?"

Mule pointed at the cryovolcano. "That's a new development. Instead of vapor, it erupted with cryomagma."

"So?"

"So, it should make you think."

"It does," Chen said. "I think you're wasting time. Our air supply will last another ten hours—fifteen if we lie down and do nothing."

"The capitalist Neptunians were brilliant innovators," Mule said. "They took big risks to make big profits. So why did they send scientists into the Oort cloud and why to Tyche?"

"You tell me," Chen said.

Mule indicated the cryovolcano. "Something is hot around here, relative to this cold place. On Triton, tidal forces cause the heat. If there was a moon circling Tyche, we'd have seen it aboard *Slovakia*. But there are no moons here. Nothing is orbiting the planetoid to cause tidal forces inside it. That means friction can't be making Tyche hot. Instead, I think the planetoid has a hot core just like Earth has, for some weird reason."

Bogdan muttered obscenities, adding, "What's your point?"

"The Neptunians built structures on Tyche because there must have been profits to make, plenty of them."

"How do profits help cyborgs?" Chen asked.

"They don't," Mule said. "You were right earlier. We're running out of air and we need a way to get close to the cyborgs without any motion sensors tracking us. Once the melds see us, we'll likely get a missile lobbed our way."

"I've been seeing explosions all around us," Chen said. "Well, in the distance anyway."

"We don't have any other choice but to attack head-on," Bogdan said. "Our mission calls for—"

"Wrong!" Mule said. "We do have choices, and the cryovolcano shows me how we can achieve tactical surprise and beat this thing."

"Start talking," Chen said. "Quit wasting our time about Neptunians."

"We've seen the geysers become more numerous," Mule said. "That means there must be a growing cryomagma-chamber below us."

"What's that?" Chen asked.

"It's where all the icy slush seethes before it comes bubbling to the surface."

"What's cryomagma?" Chen asked.

Mule pointed at the slushy semi-liquid methane. "That stuff is. We climb into the cryovolcano and work our way to the magma-chamber. That one won't be hot with lava because this isn't Earth, but freezing Tyche. My guess is the geysers and cryovolcanoes keep getting more numerous as we approach the cyborg station. That's because the magma-chamber is underneath us."

"Go underground?" Bogdan said. "You're saying we sneak up on them underground?"

"It's even better than that," Mule said. "Once we're close enough, we pop up to another volcano or vent and take a look around."

The two Marines traded glances.

"Mule," Chen said, "if this works, you're a genius."

-8-

The battlesuits weighed more than the methane liquid and cryomagma. The men sank, and sank, and the link-lines between Mule and the others was cut off. They'd probably have to be right beside each other for the link-lines to work down here.

Mule kept sinking, struck ice and deflected, skidded off more ice and kept heading down. He realized there was no way the three of them would land in the same spot. He was on his own down here underground.

A new concern struck as he kept sinking. How far down could he go? The liquid methane pressure would build up the deeper he sank.

It was dark around him, and he continued to descend like a coin tossed into a swimming pool. How deep did this chamber go anyway? The volume of cryomagma in here was incredible.

His outer armor casing began to creak. The pressure was building. This wasn't a deep-sea suit, but a battlesuit for regular conditions. Would his rifle work after this?

He chinned on his echo gear, ultrasound sonar. The suit sonar could send out ultrasound waves like a dolphin or whale on Earth. The computer would analyze the return bounce and show him on the HUD where he moved.

A red light winked. *Damn.* A feeling of despair bit him then. The sonar gear was damaged. One of the cyborg laser pulses earlier must have burned out a critical component. He instructed his computer to run diagnostics and attempt repairs or to reroute if it could.

The sonar waves would be short range down here in this cryomagma. He couldn't afford to wait for the others to find him. He had to move toward the cyborg structures, using an internal navigation system heading.

He heard his rad detector clicking. It told him he neared radioactive material. *After all this, will I die of radiation poisoning?*

He checked his dose counter. Hmm, the suit would protect him for a while, at least. He ran some analysis on the readings. It was just as he thought. This was natural material. Uranium, thorium…what if the planetoid had massive loads of fissionable material? That might be worth the mining effort, especially if the Neptunians had been able to set up an automated system.

Despite his predicament, Mule shook his head ruefully. Had he stumbled onto the Neptunian secret? Had the capitalists come out here for one of the greatest supplies of radioactive ores in the Solar System?

As his boots finally settled against something solid, he wondered if that's what the cyborgs would use as fuel. Given enough fissionable material, they might actually get this world moving. But they would need absolutely massive engines in order to do that.

Three Lurkers seemed to Mule like the outside limit the melds could sneak past the watchful Alliance. It didn't make sense that only three Lurkers could have brought enough equipment to make such gargantuan engines.

Mule waited to settle fully and then pressed down with the sole of his boot. His foot didn't slide out from under him, so likely this wasn't ice but rock. He lifted the boot and slammed it down. It didn't quite work out that way, though. The semi-liquid made it a slow-motion stomp. Still, nothing bad happened.

Am I on the bottom of the methane lake then?

He craned his faceplate upward, but saw nothing. He didn't bother turning on the outer helmet lamp. The metal casing continued to creak because of the depth pressure, but he hadn't sprung any leaks yet.

He didn't want to start walking, though, because he worried about landing on an edge or a step. If he walked over the edge or step, he might sink into an even deeper pit. Then where would he be?

No. Get started. You don't have much air left and that means you don't have any time left for hesitating.

Mule began wading through the cryomagma. He used the internal navigation system to head in the correct direction. Three times, he had to work his way around a methane iceberg. He walked, waded and resolutely continued on the mission.

An hour fled, two and finally three. The computer kept automatic track of the distance he had gone, calculating by his steps. He'd gone thirteen kilometers already, which meant he'd passed the cyborg structures.

I have to get up, but first I need a rock wall to climb.

He waded another fifteen minutes and realized he could spend the rest of his life down here, which wouldn't be long now.

A green light winked then in his faceplate and the computer informed it had made repairs. He finally had sonar again.

He began to ping objects, in particular ice and semi-frozen methane. The sonar had greater range than he would have expected down here. Once the computer configured for that, Mule spotted two man-sized metallic objects. The objects had to be Chen and Bogdan. The objects moved, and were half a kilometer away. He studied them more carefully. The two were higher than he was, much higher.

A rock wall. They must be climbing the chamber wall.

Fixing on their location, seeing it was nearer the cyborg structures, Mule began wading back the way he'd come. He kept the sonar on; it gave him sight. He found a way through an icy blockage. He also began to study the chamber walls. Here, they were exceptionally thin.

Yeah, of course: behind the magma-chamber must be other empty chambers, or corridors, thorium mining tunnels or maybe even shafts for Tyche's engines. He didn't know for certain, but it seemed logical.

Wouldn't it be dangerous having cryomagma chambers so near such shafts? It would depend, Mule decided, on what was or wasn't in the echo-empty chambers.

Mule studied the two climbers and fixed the location on an internal map. Then he shut off the sonar. It was doubtful the cyborgs above had heard the short-distance sonar, but who knew what sort of listening posts they had below ground.

Taking another careful sip of his remaining water, Mule ate a concentrate. He was tired. Despite all the practice on the gravity-wheels and in the gunner tank aboard *Slovakia*, he didn't have the same stamina he'd had on Earth. Floating in space for three years had taken its toll.

He pushed himself, wanting to get back with Chen and Bogdan. It was so lonely by himself on this planetoid of brain-stealing cyborgs. Did the men see him coming on their sonars? Or had they turned theirs off? If they'd used sonar earlier, Chen would have tried to catch him. He'd moved steadily throughout the magma-chamber, however. Likely, he'd given them a hard chase before Chen would have written him off.

It seemed to take forever, but Mule finally reached the wall the others were climbing. He began to climb, too. It was the only way out; either that, or he'd have to break through the wall between chambers, and flow out with the magma as it entered the empty places.

He'd didn't have much air left. Soon, he wouldn't be able to employ careful tactics. He'd have to charge straight at the cyborg structure, hoping it possessed more air.

Using his exoskeleton-reinforced strength, he dug his fingers into rock and kicked his booted toes in for purchase. He climbed. Once, a current caught him. He felt the sluggish magma move all around him, trying to drag him off the wall. Was there an eruption coming?

The gloved fingers of his left hand slipped out of the rock. *No! I can't afford this!* Mule silently howled in his mind. He shoved the hand back, powering his armor to *push*.

Meter by meter he crawled up, and slowly the current ebbed away. After hours of swimming, wading in the cryomagma netherworld, Mule crawled onto a shelf of sorts and squeezed his battlesuit out of a geyser vent.

He flopped onto surface ice and looked up. The stars were glorious. He laughed, the sounds echoing in his helmet. When he stopped, he crawled onto rocky ground and lay there panting.

A warning beep told him that another hour of air had been used up. That sobered him. He brought up his gyroc rifle and tried to clean it. He didn't know if it would work. If it didn't, that would leave him with pulse grenades and a vibrio-knife for hand-to-hand combat.

I have to be the reinforcement for Chen and Bogdan.

Mule spotted the two crawling toward low domed buildings. One dome was cracked and dark. Another had completely crumpled inward.

We must have done that; Captain Han's missiles hurt them.

It was good to know they'd damaged the cyborgs at least a little bit. One dome looked intact. Is that where the cyborgs had played their demonic games on the captured Marines?

Mule debated options. By their crawling speed, it seemed as if the two would have taken fifteen minutes to reach their present positions near the dome. If he crawled, it would take him too long to catch up. Because of his lack of air, he needed to leap fast. Did the cyborgs have motion sensors around here? If he began leaping, he might give the two Marines away.

Mule took out his rifle, lay down on the ice and set his HUD at extreme magnification. He'd start moving once the two men reached the dome. If they had a chance of sneaking near undetected, he was going to give it to them.

He realized this was the back side of the dome. At least, it was the back side in relation to their original vector against it. They had used the magma-chamber to go *under* the domes and come up on the other side. Was that an advantage?

Mule studied the wrecked domes and the good one. He didn't spy movement or sensors.

Just as he was about to look away, he saw a cyborg. It moved from the crumpled dome to the intact one.

He glanced at the two men. Their angle was wrong and they couldn't see the meld. It would seem the meld couldn't see them either because there was a cliff between it and the two Marines.

Mule couldn't warn them without giving away their positions. Instead, he aimed the rifle and rapid-fired. As the gyroc rockets ignited and began their flight at the enemy, Mule waited until they were halfway there. Then he got up and began to leap toward the vile cyborgs.

Mule expected the meld to whirl around before darting out of sight. It didn't. Instead, the meld dragged its left leg. It seemed sluggish and slow. At the last moment, it turned and must have registered the shells zooming at it, and then seen Mule. The thing lifted its laser pulse rifle.

Mule sailed through Tyche's weak atmosphere, willing himself to land and go to ground.

The creature raised its weapon, tracked him—then the first gyroc shell slammed against the cyborg's chest-plate. The second and third shells hit, exploding. The meld blew backward, its suit and body ruptured. Inner circuits began sparking.

Something was definitely wrong with the cyborg. That wasn't how they normally reacted. Usually they were much harder to kill.

Chen and Bogdan finally saw Mule. They stared from their prone positions.

Mule continued taking giant strides for the intact dome. As he neared, the two men climbed to their feet. Mule pointed at the dome. Because the cyborg had moved so slowly, he figured this must be their moment of opportunity. If something was wrong with the cyborgs, they needed to attack this instant. Mule swung his right arm and pointed, emphatically indicating the dome again.

Chen and Bogdan jumped and joined him: three Marines out of two thousand. None of them could use the close-channel. Their link-lines must have been damaged down in the cryo-chamber just like his. There was comm cackle on the open Marine band. It meant others still fought, but far away from here. In their powered armor, the three Marines leaped toward what looked like an intact hatch leading into the one good dome.

Mule's oxygen levels would soon be in the red. The grueling wade in the cryomagma had eaten up more of his reserves than it should have. He could tear out the hatch or he could try to open it without damage. Would cyborgs be waiting inside for them? Could the melds pry him out of his tin suit, drug him or steal his brain?

Chen landed beside him and put a gloved hand on Mule's shoulder. The sergeant's gorilla-suit gave him a nod. They were still maintaining comm silence.

Mule opened the hatch.

They stepped in, closed it and cycled air into the chamber.

Mule's guts crawled with anticipation. He gripped his gyroc.

The other two clutched theirs. Bogdan opened the inner hatch and stepped in. Laser pulses washed the front of his suit. Bogdan staggered. More pulses struck.

With a giant leap, Mule flew past the red-glowing armor and skidded on his chest-plate. He snapped off shots. The APEX rounds hardly ignited their rocket motors before slamming into cyborgs and exploding. Heat washed against Mule. Blisters rose on his skin and his air-conditioner hummed. He kept firing, as did the others.

Abruptly it was over, with hazy smoke drifting in the large dome. Suddenly, the smoke swirled and headed toward a rupture in the dome. Klaxons blared. Mule could barely hear it in his helmet.

Chen took several quick strides, picked up a metal plate and slapped it against the rupture, caused by a penetrator round ripping a hole through to Tyche's paltry atmosphere.

Climbing to his feet, Mule warily looked around. Three cyborgs lay in shattered pieces around them. It was amazing only one APEX round had ruptured the dome's skin.

The chamber was large, with hatches leading to what seemed like other rooms or cubicles. There was crated equipment stacked everywhere, and a control panel. This looked like a storage chamber, or the cyborgs had used it as one.

Chen hurried to Bogdan.

Mule spun around to look. The sub-sergeant's armor still glowed red and the Marine didn't move, but lay face down.

Chen's visor cracked open. The growth of beard, haggard skin and bloodshot eyes made the sergeant looked old and worn.

Mule did the same with his own faceplate. He wrinkled his nose at the burnt electric odors and other, more nauseating stenches. But he could breathe the stuff. He was alive and they'd found an air source.

"Let's get his helmet off," Chen said. The sergeant's voice sounded subdued in this strange dome with the dead cyborgs.

"I don't get it," Mule said, as he moved to Bogdan. "How did we outgun three cyborgs?"

"How did you kill the one outside? I don't know, but I'll tell you what I think."

Mule knelt beside Bogdan and unsnapped the emergency releases. With exoskeleton power, he popped off the helmet and wished he hadn't. Bogdan smelled like charred meat, and his features were crispy and shriveled. The lasers must have shorted battlesuit circuits and cooked the Marine like a lobster in a pot. He'd never liked Bogdan, but the man had deserved better than this.

"Damn," Chen said. "We lost a good man."

"At least Bogdan won't have to worry about them using his brain," Mule said.

Chen lifted his head as rage washed across his haggard features. "I want to kill them, Mule. I want to slaughter the lot of them."

"If the rest of the cyborgs fight as poorly as these three did," Mule said, "maybe we have a chance."

"I wouldn't count on it."

Mule raised an eyebrow.

"It was your stupid stunt that likely saved our lives," Chen said.

"You mean the magma-chamber?" Mule asked.

"I know you noticed the destroyed domes," Chen said. "*Slovakia's* drones pumped gamma and X-rays at these places. Some of the radiation must have hit some of the cyborgs. They're part machine and part man. I imagine the machine parts can take plenty of radiation, but not so much with the bio parts."

"You think radiation poisoning made them slow?" Mule asked.

"I bet the dosages would have killed us even in our suits. I think the X-rays and gamma rays were killing these cyborgs, but it was taking time. By going down and taking a swim in ice lava, and with your stunt of going off on your own… Where were you going, by the way? Why didn't you stick with us?"

"My sonar gear malfunctioned for a time. I think one of the laser burns did it."

Chen nodded. "I thought it was something like that."

"We'd better refill our air tanks and figure out our next step," Mule said. "The Web-Mind must know we made it here. It might send healthy melds after us to finish the job."

"I'll look for a compressor," Chen said. "You get me a schematic of his base. I think you're right about the Web-Mind's plan. But I also suspect we have a few minutes grace. The trouble is, I'm beginning to believe we don't have many Marines left. Maybe we're all that's left to defeat the Web-Mind and rescue our captured buddies."

Mule doubted any of the captured Marines were still alive. That wasn't the point, though. He'd made it to an air source. Now he was going to practice genocide on the Web-Mind and figure out a way to destroy every cyborg on this icy planetoid. He wanted vengeance and he wanted it today.

-9-

The panel wasn't complicated, and thirty minutes searching computer files brought up plenty of schematics and a layout of the situation. In fact, Mule believed he could piece out the situation both for the original, Neptunian plan and what the cyborgs, or the Web-Mind, intended on doing.

As he read and looked at maps, Mule's perception shifted. He quit thinking of the original scientists as Neptunians but as the Ice Hauler Cartel. That's who had been out here: cartel people or cartel employees.

He knew a little basic history. Rich individuals—cartel barons, for want of a better term—ran the icer organization. Correction, they *had* run the cartel. All those Neptunians, rich or poor, were either dead or converted into cyborgs now. Just like his wife and kids, and like all of Mars. Much of the Neptune system, or the people rather, had lived in ice-shielded habitats. Ice made an excellent insulator. The Neptunians had developed weird ice, a stronger form of ice for space construction.

The Ice Cartel had been into more than just ice, but that had been its origin. According to what Mule read, it was clear to him his guess had been right earlier: Tyche was extremely rich in fissionable ores. It had been a bonanza except for one particular. The planetoid had been much too far away from Neptune. With slow ion drives and robotic systems, it might not have been a problem. Instead of doing it that way, though—with ion-drive ore haulers and automated mining systems—the cartel had decided to bring Tyche to Neptune. Mule bet there had been other reasons for doing that, but one key reason would have been to bring the world of fissionable ores to Neptune to protect it, to keep it close under cartel guns.

The various schematics Mule brought up showed pre- and post-cyborg occupation construction. That answered one of Mule's biggest questions. How had the cyborgs bought enough equipment to build world-moving engines? They hadn't. The cartel had already shipped out those engines and had begun to install them.

By the size of pre-cyborg mines—the various sites, domes, tunnels and weapon systems—it seemed some cartel people might also have considered leaving the Solar System. Not so long ago, it looked as if nothing was going to stop the melds from conquering and converting everyone in the Solar system. In that case, Tyche would have been a humanity-filled ark. Now it was the cyborgs' turn to feel the squeeze of extinction and wish to get away. Either that or they would use the planetoid as a last ditch assault weapon against the sunbeam. The odds seemed too long to win against the sunbeam, though. It had already obliterated moons as big as this Oort cloud planetoid.

Tyche would have been more than an intergalactic ark in the making. The planetoid would have been a bonanza for the arriving cyborgs. With all the people here—it looked like several thousand had been living in pre-cyborg times—the melds could have harvested that many more meat-sacks for brains, spines and eggs and sperm. The Ice Hauler Cartel had paved the way for future cyborgs to haunt humanity into interstellar space.

"What do you have for me, Mule?" Chen asked.

They'd popped their shells. The battlesuits stood near outlets, soaking up juice and with refilled air tanks. The sergeant had been fixing faulty suit systems, at least those that he could.

Mule looked up from the panel. "It looks like Captain Han hit them pretty good," he said. "One of the X-ray missiles struck this place, which is a prime storage area. There are more storage below us in underground caverns. There's also an access tunnel leading to the main engine tunnels deeper in the rock."

"How does that help us finish the mission?" Chen asked.

"I found what must be a skimmer park," Mule said. "It's twenty kilometers from here."

"Skimmers will help us finish the Web-Mind and rescue our comrades?" Chen asked. "I don't see how."

Mule shook his head. "I'd forget about rescues missions, Sarge. Those men are already dead or wish they were. The skimmers are what we need."

"Tell me how."

"Tyche's gravity is pathetically low. We could rig a skimmer easily enough to fly out to *Slovakia*. Well, we could get an initial boost off-world and drift the rest of the way to the mothership."

Chen stared at him. "This is a suicide mission. So forget about getting home again. We're here to kill the Web-Mind and nothing else."

"Exactly," Mule said.

Chen frowned. "So how come you're talking about flying back to *Slovakia*?"

"You didn't let me finish. We don't know where the Web-Mind is. But my guess is that it's near the main engines. That strikes me as the safest place on or in the planetoid, and we know Web-Minds value personal safety above all else."

"Can we use the access tunnel to reach the engine area and reach the Web-Mind?"

"It's possible the access tunnel goes there," Mule said, "but I doubt two lone Marines can fight past the defending cyborgs."

"Our battlesuits are charged and ready. We have plenty of air and maybe more of those cyborgs are sick from radiation poisoning."

"That's too many ifs," Mule said. "I'm not interested in heroics or tough-guy fighting, I'm interesting in winning and defeating the enemy—killing them."

Chen blinked several times, and lines furrowed in his forehead. "I don't see it that way."

"It's because you're too conditioned to think things through. You want to charge in a suicidal attack when there's a better way to do this that brings us victory."

"Listen to me—"

"No, you listen," Mule said. "Two cyborgs wiped out eight Marines earlier. Who knows how many melds are left? Suppose one hundred melds are blocking our way. Can you honestly say that you can handle another hundred cyborgs?"

Chen's stubborn looked remained, but eventually he shook his head.

"I know how to kill, annihilate and destroy the Web-Mind."

"Tell me," Chen said in a ragged voice. "I'm listening."

Mule brought up a schematic. "Do you see the access tunnel's connection to the main engine tunnels?"

"Yeah," Chen said, "so what?"

"So we breach the magma-chamber." Mule tapped the schematic. "The access tunnel here is well below the magma-chamber. That means cryomagma—liquid methane—will run down the tunnel and possibly fills the engine area."

"*Possibly?*" Chen asked.

Mule silently berated himself for a bad choice of words.

"I'm only interested in *certainties*," Chen told him.

"I'm ahead of you, Sergeant. The Web-Mind will know an emergency when it's given one. I'm betting it summons all its cyborgs to stem the tide, so to speak, to stop the cryomagma flow from reaching the planetary engines."

"That saves the Web-Mind." Chen shook his head. "I want to *kill* it."

"Like I said, after we breach the magma-chamber, we head twenty kilometers away to the skimmer park. We each take one, each of them loaded with missiles. We figure out how to get them into space, fly around to the exhaust port and launch every missile we have into it. Maybe the cyborgs even have a few nuclear-tipped missiles stored at the park. It seems a likely enough place to store a few. The nuclear missiles will wreck the engines."

Chen scanned the schematics and glanced at Mule. "I'm with you as far as destroying the planetary engines. But none of your plan satisfies my need to kill the bastard of a Web-Mind."

"Sarge, if you hated someone bad enough, would you rather kill him and put him out of his misery, or would you rather lock him in a room where he had to suffer for fifty years in torment, knowing you put him there? If we destroy the planetary engines, there's nowhere for the Web-Mind to go. It's doomed."

Slowly, an evil smile spread across Chen's features. "Keep talking about torment."

***

In times past, miners had drilled the access tunnel through Tyche's indigenous rock. Moving through it sent the rad detector in Mule's battlesuit clicking like crazy. Either this was a thorium mine tunnel or it used to be.

Ahead of Mule, Chen loomed larger than normal as he carried explosives. Mule recalled a history lesson from his school days and a picture he'd seen of a Roman legionary burdened with excessive gear. The caption had been about one of Marius's "mules."

Mule's teacher back then had lectured about the ancient time and about the Roman commander named Marius, a precursor of Julius Caesar. Marius had reformed Rome's legions, letting poorer citizens become legionaries. Until then, only citizens of means had been allowed in the heavy infantry.

Marius hadn't invented or originated the new system, as much as codified what had been happening for some time. People had called his legionaries "Marius's mules" because he had done away with some of the mule allowances per certain number of soldiers. It meant each trooper carried more of his own supplies instead of shifting it onto the beast of burden. On the march, the legionaries had been loaded down like mules, and had thereby earned the nickname.

Mule also carried explosives, picked up in the cyborg structure. The two of them had enough to bring down this tunnel. They maintained comm silence, as they had been doing for some time. The link-lines were still inoperable.

Finally, Mule pointed at a spot. Chen nodded. They began using powered fists, slamming into the rock wall, punching holes deeper and deeper until they couldn't reach any farther. Only then did they stuff a hole with explosives.

Soon, dirt drifted in the tunnel so their helmet lamps washed through hazy air. They kept hammering until the Web-Mind must have decided it was time for another show-and-tell message.

"Space Marines," the emotionless voice said. "You have captured a single intact dome. It will not help you in your futile attempt to defeat me. You will end in the same situation as all your comrades in arms."

Video came to back up the boast.

Mule switched on his HUD. He saw drugged Marines on conveyers. One or two men twitched as they moved along a cyborg converter.

"No!" Chen said, switching on his comm. "Your abomination will not stand. You're a dead thing, Web-Mind. We're going to drown you."

"Ah, this is interesting." The emotionless voice almost seemed to gloat. "Another of the lice speaks?" the Web-Mind asked.

Mule motioned to Chen, wanting him to stop talking. The sergeant stood straight, glaring down the access tunnel toward the bigger tunnels that led to the planetary engines. Chen held explosives in his gloved hands, but seemed to have forgotten about blowing up the wall.

"I'm going to kill you, freak!" Chen shouted.

"How will you do that in the access tunnel?" the Web-Mind asked. "Yes, I now know where you are, mad-thing. You must travel to attack me, and you will never reach this far."

"You're wrong," Chen said. He threw down his explosives.

"Sergeant Chen!" Mule said through his comm.

"Yet another one of you lice lives?" the Web-Mind asked. "I'm surprised. But this anomaly will not last long. Even now, the situation is being rectified."

Chen roared with inarticulate rage.

"Sergeant, I've found a flamer," Mule said. "But it's too heavy for me."

Chen whirled around.

"We could use a flamer to kill the Web-Mind," Mule said.

"Yes," Chen said thickly. "Get it."

"I need help carrying it," Mule said over the comm.

"I will help you," the Web-Mind mocked—"onto a conveyer as I convert you into another of my melds."

"I want that flamer now!" Chen shouted.

Mule ran up the access tunnel toward the surface. He glanced back and saw that Chen followed him.

"You flee from me?" the Web-Mind asked. "It doesn't matter any longer, now that I know where you're hiding. I'm sending cyborgs to bring you to me."

"Where did you find a flamer?" Chen said, beginning to sound suspicious.

Mule figured he didn't have any more time to delay, as the sergeant had become too suspicious. "Get ready, Sarge."

"Ready for what?" Chen shouted.

With a remote switch, Mule ignited the explosives in the rock wall behind them. A brilliant light glowed and the tunnel, the walls, trembled as rocks and dirt rained.

"Run!" Mule shouted. "We have to get out of here before the cryomagma flows up to us and washes us down the tunnel."

The shaking worsened. It threw Mule off his feet. He got up and glided up the access tunnel, using his battlesuit at full power. He didn't dare look back because he needed to concentrate on moving. The shaking, the falling rocks hitting his battlesuit: this was like Hell.

"I'm going to kill you, Martian!" Chen raved. "You've blocked my route to the Web-Mind."

Mule didn't use the open comm anymore. He didn't want the Web-Mind to know what was in store for it. He finally glanced back, and he saw cryomagma flowing and gushing deeper into the tunnel. If the Web-Mind had sent cyborgs up the tunnels after them, the melds were about to receive the nastiest surprise of their lives.

-10-

Mule knew that one part of his plan must have worked. His battlesuit's batteries slowly and relentlessly drained as he glided in fantastic leaps across the planetoid's surface. He raced across Tyche, struggling to reach the skimmer park in time.

The amount of explosions in the distance had lessened. How many Marines still survived on this rock? The desire to find and join others was a powerful emotion. Wanting to kill the Web-Mind was an even greater desire.

This time the landscape lacked cryogeyser eruptions. They didn't spew vapor into the atmosphere. They didn't fume because the cryomagma flowed into the tunnels, draining the gargantuan chamber below the surface. Was there enough volume to drown the planetary engines and kill the Web-Mind? Mule very much doubted that. Surely, however, there would be enough magma to keep the cyborgs busy trying to stem the gushing tide.

Sergeant Chen had stopped broadcasting threats some time ago. He, too, made one powered-armor leap after another. It would have been easy enough for Chen to raise his gyroc and kill Mule. That he didn't, told Mule the sergeant had regained at least a modicum of control over his emotions.

"I have decided on a new torture for you two," the Web-Mind said. It had been silent since the magma-chamber rupture. "Ah...you have no words for me now. How very wise of you, if cowardly, Marines. You two are different from the rest. You know how to fear. Your masters must have forgotten to condition you for me."

Don't answer, Sarge, Mule thought to himself. *Don't let the devil play with your mind.*

"Fear me," the Web-Mind boasted. "Run away because you realize I am your moral superior."

Mule heard a sound in his headphones. It told him Chen had just switched on his comm-link.

"We're not running away!" Chen shouted. "We're going to destroy you."

"Indeed," the Web-Mind said.

"Sarge," Mule said. "It's trying to use you. Don't talk to it."

Over the comm-link, Mule heard Chen grinding his teeth.

"Two cowardly Marines," the Web-Mind said. "Admit the truth, at least. You flee from me."

"Nice try, cyborg," Mule said. "You think you're so smart, so wise, but we're ensuring your extinction, the death of your entire species."

"You do this by running away?" the Web-Mind asked. "That is a novel tactic indeed."

"Do you think you can trick us into telling you our plan?" Mule asked. "That shows me how desperate you are. I hope you're enjoying your magma bath."

"You are doomed," the Web-Mind said, and it sounded angry.

"You're all talk," Mule said.

"Yes, just talk," the Web-Mind said. "Enjoy my present, gnats."

Mule looked back over his shoulder. He saw a missile approaching. It streaked across the horizon for them.

"Sarge," Mule said.

"I see it," Chen said. "Yeah, I see it, Martian. It used my transmission to zero in on us. It played me for a fool." Each of them made another bound. "No," Chen said. "It isn't going to win that easily. Good-bye, Sub-sergeant, I hope you kill the thing for the two of us."

Mule wanted to shout at Chen to stay with him. But he knew there was no tricking the missile away from them. One of them had to die. Mule couldn't volunteer, because he didn't think Chen would be able to complete the mission.

Sergeant Chen veered sharply left, and he spoke on the comm. "We screwed with you, and we're going to see you become a pile of smoking ash."

Mule knew what Chen was doing. The sergeant split up, and he talked on the comm, trying to get the missile to track him. If it was nuclear, it wasn't going to matter much.

Hardening his heart to the task, Mule turned off his commlink and shouted incoherently. He leaped hard and far, stretching his bounds, trying to give himself distance. The sergeant did likewise. Neither could keep up this kind of traveling for long.

On the comm, Chen berated the Web-Mind. He laughed at it. He raved and explained exactly what he was going do with each brain.

"You have sealed your fate," the Web-Mind said.

"Good luck, Mule," Chen said. They were the last words the sergeant spoke.

The missile fell, streaking downward and reached ground level, exploding its tactical nuclear warhead.

The radiation detector clicked wildly. Mule's visor dampened the flash and he continued to leap for the skimmer park. He'd survived the tactical missile, for now. Who knew if he'd taken too many rads? If he made it back to *Slovakia* in time, he could get treatment, but first, he'd have to climb into a skimmer and get back into space. Then he had a Web-Mind to kill.

**

Sub-sergeant Mule made it to the skimmer park; what was left of it anyway. The hanger was ruined, with several skimmers mere piles of junk. He found an underground garage. There, he refilled his battlesuit's breathing tanks one more time.

He checked a working base computer and found the supplies he needed. That included a missile pod for a cargo skimmer. In the pod were three Hornet anti-missiles. The real gold mine was a Zeno nuclear-tipped missile.

Mule used a lifter and hurried the cargo skimmer to the surface. He had no idea how long it would take the Web-Mind to realize one of them still lived. A single missile to the skimmer park would end his chance at completing the mission.

He couldn't think about all the dead Marines. For all he knew he was the last human alive on this rock.

The cargo skimmer was bigger than the car used to attack them earlier. It was more like a tugboat. This must have been a Neptunian vehicle first, as it had many systems made for humans. It had an enclosed pilot space and unused gear that Mule soon reactivated. He emptied the payload area of everything he did not need and dragged in extra fuel pods.

After forty minutes hard work, he was ready. He engaged the engine, skimmed over the icy surface and began building up velocity.

"One of you is still alive?" the Web-Mind asked. It must have sensed the moving skimmer.

As the cargo hauler raced across the frozen surface, Mule pressed a switch, which activated a lone missile launcher back at the skimmer park. A missile like the ones once fired at him from a cyborg-controlled skimmer lofted from the park and headed in the direction of the Web-Mind. He hoped the missile kept the thing busy for a while.

"You are a clever one," the Web-Mind broadcast. "But it will not help you."

We'll see about that, Mule thought. Driving for escape velocity, he increased speed, and then pulled up, aiming the cargo skimmer at the stars. As he gained enough speed, he saw an explosion in the distance.

You're welcome, freak.

As he had hoped, Mule flew the skimmer off Tyche, as the sole Marine of his group left. Chen, Bogdan, Ross, Hayes: they were all dead or wishing they were.

I'll see what I can do you for guys.

Mule glanced back and saw the planetoid loom, filling his view. He kept accelerating. The skimmer reached only a pitiful speed compared to what *Slovakia* had achieved to fly out here into the Oort cloud, but at least the vehicle was getting him off the surface.

It was hard to believe he'd been lost in a magma-chamber not so very long ago. Inside his powered armor, Mule shook his head and blessed its makers, then turned his attention back to flying. It was time to concentrate and watch the skimmer controls. He would have three years to relax if he could do this right.

Within his armor, he used his chin to press battlesuit controls and inject himself with stims. Ah…the drugs felt good, and they revived him.

There came a bloom down on the surface, which might have been a launching missile. Mule watched the skimmer's radar panel. His fears materialized. The Web-Mind had sent a present after him.

Mule shut off acceleration. He'd made it into space and now coasted. Using attitude jets, he brought the stolen anti-missile pod into position, locked on, and launched one of the Hornets. It zoomed planet-ward at the upward-accelerating missile.

Mule spun the skimmer and soon accelerated away once more.

A bright splash on the radar screen showed him the Hornet had destroyed the enemy missile. Score another one for him.

A second bloom from the surface showed him that the Web-Mind wasn't finished yet. Mule knocked down that missile, too, leaving him one Hornet. It would probably come down to who had more weapons: the Web-Mind or him.

Nothing happened for a time, and Mule could see Tyche now as a ball in space. He turned to travel around it, heading for the planetoid's engine exhaust, the kilometers-wide port.

At least the Web-Mind would never strap him in a chair and torment him. Cyborgs—manmade aliens—what a vile thing for scientists to invent. He wished he could line up every scientist who had helped create cyborgs. He wished he could line up every politician who had thought making Web-Minds was a clever idea. Once they were lined up, he would walk down the row, blowing each one away. They all deserved death and worse for what they'd done. Mars was dead. The Neptune gravitational system was gone. The entire Solar System still rocked from the worst war in history.

I'm going to end it out here in the Oort cloud. It's just you and me, Web-Mind.

Mule's palms grew sweaty as the giant exhaust port came into view. He didn't wait. He didn't believe he had the time. He armed his single nuclear missile...but then hesitated.

The Web-Mind must have anti-missiles, too. The port would be the perfect place to install them.

Pressing controls, Mule fired his conventional missiles first, one at a time. As each descended for the planetoid's engine exhaust port, anti-missiles reached for them. Each of his missiles exploded long before getting to the port.

Despite the seeming futility of it, Mule aimed the skimmer at the exhaust port and dove toward the huge target. A missile rose for him.

Mule locked on and fired his last anti-missile. Seconds ticked by and there was a bloom, a hit. The last Hornet had taken out the enemy projectile.

He launched the Zeno—the nuclear-tipped missile. Afterward, he turned the skimmer at maximum, enduring the high Gs. The hope he would kill the freak elated him.

"Hey, Web-Mind," Mule said over the comm.

"Base creature. Your trickery will not help you."

Mule watched his panel. Anti-missiles rose from the port. He watched in sick despair. But the anti-missiles zoomed past the Zeno, and headed toward him.

Why hadn't the Web-Mind's anti-missiles destroyed his Zeno? Mule tried to check his own Zeno's readings. He found the missile broadcast heavy ECM, scrambling his sensors.

Finally, something has gone my way. It was a good feeling, at least while it lasted. Apparently none of the anti-missiles had hit the nuke because they couldn't find it. The Zeno's electronic countermeasures had proved themselves too powerful for the anti-missiles to achieve lock-on.

Mule didn't think the chasing anti-missiles had the range to reach him now either. He felt good again, elated, and then he thought about his wife and children. How had they felt at the end?

Mule turned on the comm. "Hey, Web-Mind," he said. "I bet I know the safest place on the planetoid. Well, should I say *in* Tyche? If I were a Web-Mind, which I'm not, I would hide by the planetary engines. That's the logical place, isn't it?"

"Self-destruct the Zeno," the Web-Mind told him.

"Say again. I couldn't get your last transmission."

"Abort the Zeno and I will return your fellow Marines to you."

"Can you give me a video image of them? I want to make sure they're all right."

"You must abort the missile now, Space Marine. If you do not…"

"I'm waiting for your boast, your threat," Mule said. "Aren't you going to tell me what a gnat I am?"

"You lack the hate-conditioning. Your voice patterns betray you."

"I'm not a pawn," Mule said, "if that's what you mean. I have free will. I'm a man, the one who's going to destroy you."

"You do not understand the crime against intelligence you are committing. You are nothing but an evolutionary dead end."

"What does evolution have to do with you?" Mule asked. "Scientists cobbled you together in their craziest moment of hubris. You're a foolish experiment gone wrong. I'm merely fixing things."

"Human, abort the missile now or—"

Mule watched the Zeno missile enter the kilometers-wide exhaust port. Seconds later, a blinding nuclear explosion blew plasma and debris out the opening.

"Web-Mind," Mule said. "Maybe you're right. I'm ready to bargain."

Static was all Mule got. Had he killed the Web-Mind? He wasn't sure. He didn't plan to go back to check. It was time to see if his cargo skimmer could reach out far enough to escape Tyche's gravity. Afterward, he would try to find and reach *Slovakia*.

***

Day 1139: Several AUs from Tyche, an emaciated, hollowed-eyed Mule lifted off an icy Oort cloud comet in Mothership *Slovakia*.

The mass tanks were full of fuel, skimmed from the comet's icy surface. Everyone in the mothership but him had died from radiation poisoning. Mule had found many of the dead at their posts, including Captain Han. Others had been curled in pain in their rooms on their cots.

He'd floated the dead into a storage chamber. Moving them while alone had been a harrowing experience.

Mule didn't know if every cyborg was destroyed on Tyche, but it seemed the Web-Mind must be. He had wrecked the engines, at least, so they weren't going anywhere. He had tried contacting surviving Marines there, but hadn't found any.

Mule didn't talk, not to himself, or the dead, or even to the ship's AI. He moved like an automaton on the mothership's bridge.

He was alive. He headed home for the inner Solar System. It would take three years to get there. He had nightmares every time he closed his eyes. He felt so alone.

But after eating his fill and taking a shower, he began to move normally again. Finally, he began speaking with the AI, making friends. It helped him send a message to Earth, to Marten Kluge, to report that the Space Marines had neutralized the cyborg menace at Tyche. Humanity could rest easy for now because brave men had given their lives in the line of duty.

After sending the message, Mule sat in the captain's chair on the bridge, staring at Sol. From this far away, it was the third brightest star after Sirius and Alpha Centauri. It was his destination, well, the Inner Planets. Mule wondered what awaited him at the end of the voyage. Then he closed his eyes, thinking once more about his lost people, his vanished wife and children. On their graves he vowed that if there were more cyborgs left, he was going to find them—and annihilate every one.

The End

SF Books by Vaughn Heppner:

DOOM STAR SERIES:
Star Soldier
Bio Weapon
Battle Pod
Cyborg Assault
Planet Wrecker
Star Fortress
Task Force 7 (Novella)

EXTINCTION WARS SERIES:
Assault Troopers
Planet Strike
Star Viking
Fortress Earth

INVASION AMERICA SERIES:
Invasion: Alaska
Invasion: California
Invasion: Colorado
Invasion: New York
Invasion: China

Visit www.Vaughnheppner.com for more information.

Printed in Great Britain
by Amazon